Enthrall

THE FOUND BY YOU SERIES: BOOK FOUR

VICTORIA H SMITH

One

ANDIE

THE SWAYING OF THE HIPS, and the movement of the bodies always seemed to fascinate me most. Every girl did it differently, tailored individually to the customer she aimed to please. That was our specialty of course, individuality. At *Club Prestige* we valued our patrons, and they paid us very handsomely to do so.

That detail set us apart from the rest – the perfectionism. Each girl studied her assigned patron, as did our male dancers. We had female members, too. After all, the men couldn't have all the fun.

I nodded at Chloe through the two-way mirror. She knew I was there. Whenever I swept the area, a red light ticked on at the top of the door, signaling to the dancers. I needed to know they were okay and didn't need anything. That was my job as head of security.

She fluttered her fingers above her, sporting a nice bit of black lingerie. A wink of her lengthy lashes allowed me to move on, as well as let her patron enjoy his private dance. As I walked away, I saw his head lay onto the back of the lounge chair.

I pushed my hands into the pockets of my little black dress, one stiletto after the other as I circulated the room. The Onyx Room: a labyrinth of many, and one of my favorites. The room's set up was two major sections: a male designated area, and female designated area, though some nights intermingling was allowed. Tonight was one of those nights, but for the most part, people had a tendency to keep to their areas. The entire space was surrounded by over a dozen other smaller rooms, and various hallways to guide our guests to each. I enjoyed the privacy of it, the secrecy. Each room held its own, and again, was individualized to whoever paid for a section. Some bought fifteen minutes, others, hours at a time; we even had an overnighter once, which we didn't usually do here. But if the price was right...

Another nice feature was the two-way viewings only myself and my team had access to. It helped to do my job more efficiently, and I was all about efficiency.

Standing, I waited for Gerard to open the private door letting us out into the common area. We had the standard set up there: lounges, drinks, dancing. A person could rent out the entire room for a party, and use the smaller ones for more "intimate" gatherings, usually lap dances, what Chloe was busy doing.

I blended in. Gerard and Mason, however, looked like security. But we didn't mind. It helped set a nice tone in the room. The male patrons knew they were there, and that allowed things to flow more easily for both dancers and members alike.

A member arose from his chair, raising his drink, and cutting me off when I attempted to scoot by. The room's soft lighting blanketed his face into an ombre, making light-colored eyes darker. He enveloped me, asking me if I wanted to join him in a room.

I wasn't surprised by the invitation, of course. That was

the point of the little black dress. In the male-only designated sections of *Prestige*, I resembled just another dancer, and the female sections, I seemed like a member to the Club.

From across the room, Gerard gestured to Mason, who was just a few tables distance from me.

I lifted my fingers causally, allowing them to stay unconcerned. There was a reason I was head of security. If I wanted to, I could take down a grown man with a few strategically placed maneuvers. Gerard and Mason both knew that, but they always offered the option of their services.

They held their ground, and I did what I do best.

I moved. Swaying hips, and, though not individualized to this man, they seemed no less mesmerizing to him. That told as his arms moved around me, hovering, as I danced in front of him. Sometimes old school just worked, and training never left you.

Once I was done, I lifted a perfectly polished nail to his cheek, told him *maybe next time,* and left him standing there amongst the group he was with. His cheeks puffed out, his arms lowered, and his drink seemed to be strategically placed in front of a sizable erection through his pleated pants.

This girl's still got it.

Smiling, I let the boys lead me to sweep our next section. The female-only area never usually had its excitement, but then again, the male area didn't either. We had a different type of clientele here. Ladies and gentlemen's clubs tended to be that way.

We circulated quickly, peeking into occupied rooms through the two-way mirrors, and ignoring the empty ones. Gerard kept the roster. They were all accounted for and filled with the appropriate party. We were about to head back to the male section, but my vision caught an outlier.

I lowered the roster Gerard had handed to me, spying a suit that didn't look familiar to me. I squinted at this oversized man with a thick, coarse beard. He stood about ten feet away, hands folded in front of himself as he watched over the area. He also stood directly to the side of a sub-room with sunglasses on his face, though the area was more than dark.

I tilted my head back. "He's not mine."

Gerard and Mason panned over to his general direction.

"He could be security for a patron," said Mason.

I narrowed my eyes. We had no rules against that here. If our patrons felt it necessary, we complied, but I was always aware of that fact.

I wasn't aware of this.

I headed over, my team and I easily catching the attention of the guard. He eyed me when I made my way, tilting his head to gaze at me over his sunglasses. I noticed two soft dimples appear in the corner of his dark skin, so I played along. I had to figure out who he was guarding.

I grazed his lapel; my ruby-red nail contrasting his all black suit. He easily let me move past him.

That was, until I tried to open the door.

His hand went out, deterring my next move. Mason and Gerard stiffened.

I raised my hand.

"I need by," I said, touching that lapel again. "Now why are you giving me such a hard time, big boy?"

The words tasted like putrid vomit in my mouth, but I let them flow.

The big guy's gaze left my team; his head lifting let me know that. He lowered his dark shades to me again.

"You work here?"

Quirking my red lips to the side, I smiled, pointing my thumb behind me.

"Why do you think they look like they want to kill you?"

The man smirked, then nodded, stepping aside to let me

in. The boys looked as if they wanted to follow, but the big guy moved closer to me, cutting them off.

I really don't need this right now.

I waved them off, and then made my way in. I knew this particular room to be vacant tonight, so the fact that the big guy in the suit felt so protective over the area had me highly suspicious.

I made my way, pushing through black chiffon draping that hung from the rafters, and shimmering matching carpet. These elements were supposed to be here for tomorrow's booking, but the sounds, *the moans*, shouldn't be.

My vision reddened the louder the moans got, even though I, pretty much, knew what I was about to come across, but that didn't stop me. It was my job to stop shit like this.

To control shit like this.

I saw a body first—a naked female thigh. My gaze followed her skin up to brown ass cheeks, again naked, and bouncing on top of a lap. As crazy as it sounded, I recognized it before even seeing her face. She was one of my girls. The unique volcano-red silken hair told me that.

She was the one moaning. Her naked breasts being fondled by a set of dark hands—large ones that connected to chiseled arms and firm biceps. He wasn't naked though, this guy. His thick upper half exposed only part way, his white t-shirt lifted slightly, revealing a set of dark abs the tone of a rich and shiny marble.

His head was back, his mouth open, but not for my girl. No. He had another one who had her tongue down his throat. She was also naked, but I had no idea who she was; her soft pink tits on full display for anyone who wanted to see.

The guy reached one hand off my girl. Doing so allowed him to fondle both women's breasts at the same time, and I knew right away who had control of this situation - who *instigated* this situation.

A scream sounded the minute I pulled my girl off of this man's lap. This exposed right away a pretty sizable dick, which made me laugh internally. I would have guessed he wouldn't be packing. Men who needed two women usually needed to overcompensate for a reason.

"What the hell—" His eyes, already large, went wide.

What a damn shame I thought, as I studied a sharp jaw line and full lips. The best looking ones always tended to be the biggest assholes.

He pushed his glistening dick away, taking only a moment to pull off the condom stretched over his length. He tossed it in the trash beside the lounge.

"Who are—"

The door behind us shot open. I swear, that dark skin of his went pale upon seeing Mason and Gerard quickly flanking my sides.

"Ms. Simmons—!"

I grabbed my girl's shirt up off the floor. She already had her underwear back on, and was attempting to get her skirt up. I pushed the shirt into her chest, covering her nakedness.

"My office—now." We were going to have a little talk about this—she knew the rules here.

Chewing her lip, she left the area.

The guy was pulling his shirt down. My men let him do so before grabbing him by the arms. They got him up on his feet and he towered over them both; and that was saying something, both my men were at least six-three.

"Hey!" he said, struggling, but at this point resistance would do him no good against two former CIA. His gaze caught mine.

"What are you—?"

I stepped up to him and he silenced. Honestly, I had no idea why, but he did. His gaze moved over me, those brown eyes on mine. His nostrils flared a bit, and a breath escaped his lips from his broad chest. I stepped back.

Once I did, my team moved him past me. I held my hand up, signaling them to wait. I reached down to grab a white envelope I spotted on the floor.

I slipped it into the man's shirt pocket, assuming it was his. My eyes narrowed, and this time, I didn't step away.

He was watching me; those eyes circulating. That was until I severed his glare, motioning for my boys to take him away. They did so efficiently.

"Please make sure he and his friend never enter my club again," I said. I trusted that my guys took the initiative to have his security restrained behind me, and I realized I didn't care who that man was to have such a guard. He broke the rules. He broke the rules, so he was out.

As they left the area, I was left with the guy's other partner. She had her clothes on by now, and watched me as I stepped up to her.

I put my hands behind my back.

"What party are you here with?" I asked, my stare unfaltering.

She swallowed. "The Emerson Party."

I knew it well. Again, I memorized every event.

I nodded.

"Please inform Ms. Emerson her membership has been revoked for a month as consequence, and that her current event is now over for the evening."

I left her there, her jaw slacked, and I reached for the door.

"But it's her bachelorette party," she pleaded, her voice so small behind me. She seemed very upset, but I simply kept on.

I had rounds to do.

Two

D

"You did *what*?"

My boy Griffin's tone cut like a knife. They said I did something wrong. They said I fucked something up. We had planned for weeks—hell, *months.* I knew I couldn't easily come back from this.

What else was new?

Letting out a breath, I fell back on to the lounge in my hotel room. I hadn't even bothered to fly back home to Chicago yet. I guess I'd been in too much shock from what went down.

Being thrown out of an upscale club will do that to a guy.

I push my hand over my head, my fingers grazing the buzz of my bald fade haircut. I leaned forward, phone in hand.

"I kinda, sorta lost the venue."

He was silent for too long. Maybe even longer than when I originally called and blurted out the news.

But then he chimed in.

"So when you say you lost the venue..."

That lazy drawl of his took a second. I usually made fun of him for it. My favorite was telling him that he sounded like a missing Beverly Hillbilly—especially when he was around his family back in Texas. Giving him a hard time about his accent was easy, and I guess just came with the territory of the whole "best friend thing."

I wouldn't dare do that shit right now.

I started again before he could finish.

"I mean, we don't have it *anymore*—"

"Why?"

I swallowed.

"Well, we've been... banned. In a sense." At least, that's what I assumed when I was thrown out. They told me not to come back and I figured that was pretty much a given. I guess the real person I had to answer to was Griffin's teammate, Taylor. He held the actual membership at *Club Prestige*, and got Griff access as a guest for us to plan an event there.

I had to answer to one person at a time at this point.

"D..."

"I went there like you said," I hurried, patting the air with my hand as if he was here to calm.

"I went to pay the deposit and check out the space."

"So how did... *that* turn into you losing the venue?"

He rushed those last few words like a simmering pot of water ready to bubble over.

So I rushed, too.

"Uh, so what went down was..." Obviously I'm not too good at rushing.

I swallowed again.

"I got a little *into* the place, and it's a nice place, Griff. Real good for a party—"

"D."

I breathed.

"I ran into this chick."

Well, two, but he didn't need to know that.

"And she...erm, she kind of worked there. We went into

one of the rooms and things kind of got a little out of hand. Anyway, security caught us, and I don't think they like that. They must have had a 'no touching' policy or something."

Like most clubs did, I supposed, especially one of that caliber.

Damn.

"What the actual *fuck*, Diondre!"

I pulled a breath through my teeth, actually feeling the cut of those words. But then another voice came in, a softer one, a nicer one in the distance.

"Griffin..." she said, and I knew it was his fiancée, or I guess now his wife, Roxie.

The pair were actually on their honeymoon as we spoke, something they more than deserved. They decided to take it more than half a year after the actual wedding, both of them caught up in the business of their lives.

Griffin, like myself, played professional basketball. Also, like myself, was a hot commodity on his team in Miami; though, he climbed the ranks a little quicker than I had in our short, year-long careers. The guy was all over the place after his point guard injured himself in Griffin's rookie season. He essentially took over for the guy, and even though his point guard was back on his feet, Griffin's life only slowed a little. He was still a wanted man, busy, and from what I heard, things for Roxie were no different. She'd recently enrolled in law school, though I had no idea what she'd be doing with that. I just knew they did a lot of reading and shit, so she must have been busy.

I waited, chewing anxiously on the inside of my cheek while I sat anxiously during their exchange on the other side of the world. They were literally on the other side of the world— Fiji to be exact.

I couldn't hear exactly what, but Roxie did say something, and after she had, Griff breathed into the phone.

"Sorry, baby," he said, his voice suddenly the utmost of calm. She had that effect on him, his Roxie.

"He's just frustrating as shit."

I guess even she couldn't make magic happen. I fell back to the lounge again, facing out my window at the busy streets. My agent got me a high-rise in a badass hotel. Too bad I couldn't enjoy all DC had to offer.

I was too busy getting reamed.

"Griffin," I started, choosing my words more carefully, "this isn't so bad. We can find another place."

"Really?" he asked, but something told me he wasn't really asking.

The word dripped in sarcasm.

"How are we supposed to do that on such short notice? We've had this party planned for months, D. *Months.*"

He was really being generous with that. What he meant to say was *he* had this party planned for months. He was good at stuff like that: responsibility.

"We had everything secure, everyone secure," he continued, "we even got Ryan's brothers to come out for this thing."

Which I knew was no easy feat. Our friend's brothers were in the military. More specifically, stationed in Japan. But Griffin made it happen for them to come out to Ryan's trade party. The party was for our old college roommate Ryan to celebrate his trade to DC. Like us, he played professionally, and finally got the team he wanted, which was in the District of Columbia, his hometown. He finally got to come home, which made me feel even more like an idiot.

I slid my hand down my face.

"We can make this work."

"You're right," he went on, "we can make this work because you will."

"Griff—"

"You're going to fix this, D," he said. "You're going to fix this because you messed up, and I don't care how much ass you have to kiss to do it. Get us back in our space, and do it quickly. Ryan would do this for either one of us, and you know that."

I did. Outside of Griff, he had it the most together. He always had.

"I'll fix it," I promised him. And I would. I swore I would.

"Good. I'll talk to you later, okay? Roxie and I are going to the beach."

I smiled a little. I never felt like I wanted something like that—a girl permanently on my arm—but my boy kind of made it sound good sometimes.

Only some.

I let him go, promising him again I would fix this, and tossed my phone on the bed.

Pushing my hand back over my face, I watched the television I had put on mute when I finally got the nerve to call Griff. My eyes traveled over what was clearly news with no absorption of the information in front of me what-so-ever. My mind was racing.

How had I let this happen? I saw that girl and I...

I pulled shit like that all the time—and had well before playing professional ball, too. When it all came down to it, I let my cock do the thinking, which wasn't so bad when it was just me I had to think about. But Griffin had given me one job to do—pay the deposit and check out the space.

I cursed, trying to figure this out. I wasn't really sure what could get us back into *Club Prestige*. I had money, but I had a feeling that wouldn't work for this kind of place. I mean, you practically needed a body scan just to get in. The place required a membership, and if not, a word from a member to gain access. Of course, we had that with Taylor, who I assumed frequented the place. He came from old DC money, and this place screamed it. Money didn't push at a place like that, influence did, which a once poor kid from the south side of Chicago, didn't have.

I turned the sound on the TV up absentmindedly, tossing the remote on the hotel room's coffee table after. Maybe I could convince Griff to change locations. But he was right. This event was *big*, and we'd made sure to hit up all of Ryan's buddies. This was all for him. This was all about him.

But I'd somehow made it about me.

Shaking my head, I turned toward the television, distracted by some guy that struck me as familiar.

I turned up the program, the guy on the screen crowded by people. Most of them had sunglasses on, and escorted the guy out of a courthouse. In front of the party, reporters shoved microphones in the dude's face, which his entourage quickly pushed away. I read the headline scrolling along the bottom of the screen:

"Washington Shooting Guard Tucker 'Tuck' Simmons Charges Dropped."

My eyebrows flickered up. Seeing the name struck a sudden awareness. This guy and I hung out in the same circles, had acquaintances. In fact, I'd seen him at quite a few parties. I partied a lot, and though, I didn't really know him, I did know him to be a little bit of a big deal. He was recruited to DC out of high school, barely nineteen, from what I remembered.

I scratched my chin, shaking my head a little as I read with the scrolling text. It seemed the hotshot was already getting himself into trouble, a DUI.

Smirking, I palmed the remote. He better be careful with that shit. Trouble this early on in his career *and* at such a young age...? I didn't want to say this guy didn't have a shot, but...

I knew firsthand how bad things could get when you got in over your head.

I went to turn the channel, move on, but stopped the minute I saw something, the minute I saw *someone.*

A pair of black boots zipped all the way up caught my attention. Creamy brown thighs filled them deliciously, like a fine wrapper to toffee. She was nothing but fine to look at. Like some kind of damn masterpiece in the way she moved in that tight dress of hers, like a second skin formed over thick thighs and large breasts. The entire outfit was black, which contrasted all the colorful, gaudy shit around her. The dude's entourage looked like a circus. The kid wore an oversized rainbow shirt and sweatband around his head.

Fuckin' kids.

I couldn't see the girl's eyes, as they were hidden behind dark sunglasses, but that didn't matter. I remembered them well. They were a smoked brown, deep and wide with so much going on within them. I was sure lots of that had been about me and that wasn't my ego talking. She'd been at the forefront of the entourage that kicked me out on my ass, those eyes on me the whole time; I'd never forget them. They were very hard to forget. She was very hard to forget, hell, with how interesting she looked. Her entire head was buzzed, a cut even shorter than mine, with hazel-toned hair.

I'd never seen anything so sexy in my life; the confidence she had to rock a style like that.

I watched her, in the background of this kid, but very much supporting him. It was like she was trying to blend in, and doing it well. Who was she to him? A girlfriend, or...

And then her hand went to his back—only slightly, and only for a moment, but it said so much before she pulled away —something like, "I'm here. I got you."

The guy's name flashed on the screen again, but I didn't know what it was.

But hell, it sure did click something.

"Ms. Simmons!" the girl at the club said that night—the name of her superior.

Tucker 'Tuck' Simmons, the television read. I sat back, watching the pair get into a black SUV with tinted windows. Before it took off, the kid rolled down the window and pushed his middle finger out toward the crowd. He yelled something just as colorful as his shirt to the reporters before pulling away. Something else clicked.

I think I just figured out how we're getting our venue back, or at least, a way to talk to the person who took it all away.

Three

ANDIE

This was my second time doing this with Tasha. The first time had been the night I found her.

She'd been bouncing on a dick at that time.

The second was now. She'd come to my office to get her last check, and I had just as little patience for it now as I did the other night.

I flipped a page in the dossier I had been studying, sighing before gazing up. The glass panes of my corner office highlighted the panic in her brown eyes. She had a similar look the night of her lapse in judgment, a fear that told me she had no idea how she'd pay that next bill, or how she'd feed herself now.

I closed the dossier, my acrylics clacking against each other when I folded my fingers.

"You know the rules, Tasha. You broke them, so you're out." She was lucky all I was doing was firing her, not pressing charges. *She* may have worked here, but that other girl didn't. They'd both put themselves in a terrible position. A potentially dangerous position that could have been far worse than a quick thrill with a basketball player.

Yes, I knew who he was, hence the full dossier underneath my fingertips. His name was logged the minute he entered my club.

Diondre Combs - bench warmer for the Indiana Pacers, though I had a feeling that was a matter of his career being in its infancy. He'd only been playing for a short period of time, and from what I had gathered about his stats, he was actually quite good. But he couldn't expect to go too far if he continued with the kind of stunt he pulled in my club. Come to find out, he was actually supposed to attend an event we had later in the week, hosted by one of our members.

I had to hand out a lot of suspensions along with Ms. Emerson that night. Taylor Charles hadn't been happy to hear that, as he was actually one of our more esteemed members. He never caused trouble and it had been a shame I had to crack the whip on him. I did a standard suspension, a few months, and as Mr. Charles only visited every few, it would be lifted before he even came back out. I think that had been the only reason he hadn't been more upset.

Oh, God, she's crying now.

I lifted from my desk, swaying over to the sobbing dancer in my office. I ripped a tissue out of the box on my desk.

"Tasha, please don't make a scene." I didn't particularly enjoy making people cry. Especially when all I was trying to do was protect my girls - even if it was from themselves.

She accepted the tissue, pressing it to her flooding eyes hidden behind red-tipped hair.

"I... I..." she hiccupped.

I sighed again, leaning on the edge of my desk.

"It's for the best, Tasha. I'm sure with your next job you'll think about what happened here," and hopefully make better decisions.

Turning away, I pulled a white envelope from under Diondre's dossier. It would be the last time I read the thing. I had no more interest in him after I found out his purpose for being in my club, and handed out the proper consequences.

She blew her nose. It was a long one that made me purse my lips. She rubbed a nostril with the tissue. "I'm going to bring this up with the other owners."

I fought the urge to lift my eyes to the ceiling. "I own one-fifth of this club, and my colleagues support my decisions, as I do theirs. My decision stands, and you're only making things worse for yourself the longer you stand here and insult me in my own office. Now please, take your check and leave."

She had no right to attempt to step over my stake in this business, this company. I may have once been like her, but I changed things for myself.

I made things happen for myself.

The initial sweet, sobbing girl in my office faded before me when she took her check. As we made eye contact, her eyes narrowed and became even colder. Flipping red locks over her brown shoulder, she turned away.

"You're such a bitch," she snapped, then slammed my door, causing my framed art to sway.

She was wrong about that though. I was her friend, which was why I was firing her. That night with Diondre could have turned out far worse.

Sighing once more, I called Mason, my number one, into my office. He slid me a folder from under his beefy arm, knowing the routine. I thanked him before taking it back to my desk.

I had one thing to handle first.

Diondre's dossier hit the bottom of my trash can with a thump, and I found I could breathe again. The trash was now properly disposed of.

I quickly went into my routine, thumbing through the

folder Mason gave me. It had the list of that evening's events, and though I already had them memorized, I studied them again. When I had finished, I called both him and Gerard back in. We went over the extra security measures we were getting ready to install in the upcoming weeks. In all honesty, my team had this place more than safe, but I'd had a meeting with the other owners this morning, and the extra security measures were agreed upon. The measures were more a show of strength; a stand, that we here at *Club Prestige* were here to stay, and wouldn't be threatened. We'd had an amazing first year with more success than we knew what to do with.

Which was, I supposed, why our neighbors disliked us so much.

Something about not wanting a club of our... *type* in the neighbor. Our legal team was handling the particulars. I just had to keep the club's security on the up, which of course, I had no problem handling.

Smiling over the current plans for the new measures, I stood from my desk, handing Mason back the folder.

"Excellent, gentlemen."

They nodded, all smiles themselves before turning to head out of the room. But I had one more matter to bring up as I retook my seat.

"Did the car I secured for Mr. Simmons for this evening deliver him to his location as I requested?" I asked, pulling my chair under my desk. Of course, the car had, but I always verified.

I received a nod from Mason.

"Yes, Ms. Simmons. I delivered him myself to the party he requested drop off to, though I did advise him the safety of the location was less than desirable."

My eyes narrowed.

"I'm sorry - how is a party at one of the nicest hotels in town an 'unsafe location'?" In fact, it had been like pulling teeth just to get him to agree to go to it, and not some shady establishment where he usually liked to hang out with his less-than-desirable friends.

My brother could be rather disagreeable.

Now, it was Mason's eyes that narrowed.

"That's not where he had me deliver him, ma'am. He went to a party in the glades, at South Hill to be exact."

My brother had officially lost his mind.

Four

D

Hotshot showed up, just like I thought he would. I wasn't surprised. My boy Q threw some of the best house parties.

That was, if you were willing to venture into the hood to get to them.

That's how Q started I supposed - the hood. He operated his fine jewelry business right out of his basement. His pieces were outstanding, and I copped quite a few myself. I wasn't the only one - dude was known all over the country. I was about ninety percent sure that's what got the rookie over to these parts.

I guess I spread the word well.

I tipped my Corona back, watching him as I shook my head. The guy had a chick on either side of him, clearly trying to impress the room with his arm candy for the evening. Dude needed validation, I guess.

He was wearing another one of those damn clown shirts.

He had his hands above his head now, grinding up against the ladies with his tongue hanging out of his mouth. I lifted my eyes to the heavens.

What a damn tool.

He looked just as much on television, though I liked to give a guy the benefit of the doubt. One thing I knew about the media was they liked to get a man at his worst, but what I was witnessing now seemed like a pretty accurate portrayal. The song playing throughout the house changed over to something else, and it must have broken the guy's flow because he stopped dancing, taking his girls over to couches. They sat next to him, one on each side, looking far more interested in the man on the *other* side of the couch, but I wouldn't blame them for that. Q was a pretty fly dude, and Hotshot, taking his seat beside him with his girls, got the attention of Q and his boys crowded around. They all chatted for a bit, and oddly the kid held Q's interest enough to do so.

I brought my gaze away from the exchange a bit, finding myself doing that more and more as the evening progressed. The kid showed up like I hoped, but I didn't fail to notice he arrived short one buzz-haired bombshell.

Where was his girl? The one from the club? I mean, that *had* to be her relation to him: security. She kept the paparazzi and reporters back like some kind of CIA on television, and let's not forget her appearance at the club. She came in and shut shit down, no holds barred, which any other time, I'd say was kind of hot, empowering and shit if I hadn't been the one with my pants down...

I sure did get my ass handed to me that night, didn't I?

Smiling a little, I shook my head, sipping more of my Corona against the wall. There were a few things that really had me confused as hell about her. She had all kinds of questions buzzing around in my head about who she was. The main one being her role to the kid besides security. The pair *did* share a last name - that much I gathered - but I still wasn't sure about the connection. She could be anything from a spouse, to his mom. That first one had my beer tasting like bile in my mouth. She didn't look old enough to be his mother, though. She looked to be in her twenties, like me.

Hotshot had his head thrown back now, looking dopey as hell as he threw two arms around his ladies and chuckled at something Q said. He even had his tongue hanging out of his mouth during the laugh. His clown shirt only cemented what a jackass this guy was.

I smirked. I refused to believe a woman of that caliber had a claim staked on her by anyone, let alone the kid on the couch. He wouldn't be able to handle her. Nah, not in the slightest.

She'd even given me a run for my money.

Smiling again, I continued to circulate the room with my gaze, but had a feeling I might be left empty tonight. The kid came minus not only her, but any security detail at all, so maybe he decided to pull solo. Tonight, my only hope was staying until this thing closed out, and maybe being able to catch Mystery Girl, if she was his ride.

"Fuck yeah, Q!"

The eloquent sentence was followed by another douchy laugh, and I lifted my eyes to the heavens. I hoped... *Ms. Simmons* arrived soon. I didn't know how much more I could take of this babysitting shit.

Giving the kid another look, I watched him reach for Q's hand. My boy had it extended to him for some reason. I quickly discovered it was to pull him into him, the pair exchanging a shake and a hug. The kid ended it with a snap, and Q rose from the couch, the kid's attention going back to his girls immediately after.

My eyes narrowed at the scene, then lifted when I realized Q was coming towards me. He reached for me, shaking my hand, before pulling me into a one-armed hug.

"'Sup, man?" I said, patting his back.

He stepped back, tipping his chin at me before grabbing himself a Corona off the bar I stood near.

"Ain't got nothing to complain about," he said, and I heard that.

I smiled.

"Life is good, and I thank you for this thing tonight." In fact, he'd had a pivotal role in getting the kid here - him and his connections. Q had friends all over the city, and was able to get the word out right to him. I guess the kid had been headed to some ritzy party at a hotel tonight before he was redirect by a phone call. Q knew everyone.

"Kid seems to be having a good time," I told him, tilting my drink that way. Q nodded his head of dreads, and chuckled.

"No problem. He ain't so bad."

I supposed I hadn't actually spoken to the kid to gauge that, but I figured any guy who walked in with two chicks wearing a clown costume wouldn't be much of a conversationalist.

Shrugging a little, I put my judgment aside and took another swing. If Q said he was 'aight he probably was.

Another guy in a room across the hall caught Q's attention as he lifted a tumbler of brown liquid at him. Q returned it with a salute of his own drink, and I figured my time was about to be up with the guy. That was confirmed when he brought me in again. Another shake, then a hug.

"Look me up when you roll through Chi-Town again," I told him, more than happy to hook him up with some game tickets.

We could have a good time.

"Sure thing," he said, "and feel free to invite the kid anytime to these things. He's cool people and I can't wait to do business with him."

I took a drink.

"Is he buying some of your pieces or something?" That would explain their exchange before. Q's jewelry work was some of the finest.

He grinned a little. "Nah, I'm actually buying some of his. He's got word on a shipment coming in. Guns and other things."

The last sentence had me turning my head, eyeing Hotshot again. That's the last thing I ever would have thought a rookie like that would have his hand in. But again, if Q was saying it...

I let my mind linger, finishing my beer. I left the rookie on the couch to dispose of my bottle, and headed back to my station right after.

But there was a slight interception.

She wandered the house. Blocking the hall I would have taken from the kitchen back to the kid, those heels made their rounds. She stamped the carpet with charged steps, thick thighs. The tiniest waist flared off into hips easily exposed if done just right, as well as a tight green dress that only needed a slight turn of the hand...

I went around a couple of people dancing, not losing sight of her. I could have easily approached her, but instead, just watched her a little, taking a seat on the edge of an end table. Ms. Simmons had her eyes on the room tonight, a set of keys in her hand. The woman damn-near glided. Something in her eyes made me seriously question using that hand. I could slide easily between those sweetened brown thighs and bring her out of the determination that held her gaze. She was clearly looking for someone.

Maybe she just needed to find him.

I got up, moving with her at a distance, but the closer I got, the closer I could see her. I guess that would be the point, but something slowed me. A slight tint touched her cheeks, her face flushed all over, and pinked lips worried in the corners. She did look worried, which was a far cry from the previous time I'd seen her - unrelenting, self-assured. And then a word came out of her mouth.

"Tucker?" she said, pushing past a couple, and then another.

"Tucker?"

I followed her, again staying at a distance, for the most part, until I found myself right up on her. She'd stopped for a moment in her search, holding onto a wall as she stood up on the toes of her heels. Hotshot's name left from her lips once more, and I reached out toward her. I didn't know what I was going to do; tell her I knew where he was, or what, but I found I had to do something. She looked so damn worried.

Her pivot choked my words down.

I think she meant to redirect her search, but in her reroute, she hit me, and almost lost her balance. She got me full on, hands on my shirt, and her in my arms.

As I unraveled her from my grasp, my hands rested on her shoulders. I brought them down skin that was butter smooth, and so hot to the touch.

She gazed up at me, dark brown lashes contradicting her buzzed, caramel hair, and she said another name. But this time, it wasn't the kid's.

"Diondre?" she gasped, unblinking, making my brow jump.

Some people pushed behind her, trying to get past her I was sure, but all that did was press her up against me. Soft breasts kept her shapely hips from getting any closer, and thank God for that.

So hard in my jeans, I held her back a little, noticing more than beaded nipples through her thin dress.

"Eh, um," I jumbled, and I didn't jumble—ever.

I blinked.

"Yeah," I stuttered, answering her. "But I don't think I got your name."

Had she looked me up?

Like she realized her slip up, her eyes went wide, and suddenly narrowed.

Then they went cold.

She flew out of my hands like she'd never been there, and then those heels pivoted again. They headed in the opposite direction of me this time, and maybe if she hadn't been trying to get away from me she would have noticed the guy trying to get her attention at the wet bar.

His hand going for her ass came down with a *crack* and I'd never seen someone whip around so fast.

She clearly got to him before I could.

I was only mid-fist raised when she swung around and had her elbow against this guy's throat. Using her heel as leverage, she had this guy up against the wall, and those eyes narrowed even harder.

"You don't touch me," she growled. "*Ever.*"

His cheeks puffed up, his face going white, and I seriously thought she'd kill this guy right here in the middle of the living room. By now, she'd gathered a crowd, and seemed no closer to letting this man go. I mean, it had been a fucker's move for sure - putting his hands on her - and if she hadn't gotten to him, I know I would have had him on the floor just out of sheer principle. I had two sisters myself, and I never put my hands on a woman unless she was giving me the body language to do so. That would have been the end of it though. A quick punch...

I put my hand on her shoulder again.

"Hey," I said, my breath expelling if not just a little. I couldn't help it by what she was doing to this guy. She could cut off his air supply only too easily. She could kill him.

She didn't let go immediately, and I squeezed her shoulder

just a little. When I did, she finally let go. It had been slow -
but she did. She stepped back like she got her head together,
and a random name, "Andie" had her gaze panning to the
couch. It went to the same couch I left the kid on.

"Tuck."

She fell from my hand again, leaving me standing there,
and I watched her head over to the kid, looking flabbergasted
in the middle of Q's living room.

He eyed her.

"What the..." But then he gazed around, and something
about what he saw made his eyes change.

His jaw stiffened. "What the *fuck* are you doing here?"

I blinked. What was his problem, and why would he say
such a thing to her, like she couldn't take his ass down in the
middle of this house?

Watching her, I half expected her to. He'd clearly disre-
spected her, but she didn't. If anything, I saw her shrink two
whole sizes where she stood.

She sighed a little. "I came to find you. You didn't go
where you said you'd be and left your security detail. I mean,
what were you thinking?"

His eyes lifted and he stumbled a little, going back to the
couch. Retaking his seat, he got comfy and put his arms
around the ladies he brought with him.

"I don't answer to nobody," he said, then opened his
mouth to a lit blunt. One of his girls had one, and slid it right
between his lips.

"Andie" reached over and ripped it right out.

"The fuck, Andie—!"

She stamped it out with her heel. "You need to get up and
get out of here. Do you even know these people?"

When he pushed away from his girls he sent them flying
back. He got up in Andie's face. "You need to back the hell off—"

Hotshot watched as I got between them, but I didn't do it in an aggressive way, assessing the situation first. This guy would be an idiot to think that had anything to do with him though. My interception had very much to do with her, and how horrified she'd be if I punched this little fucker in his jaw if he said one more wrong thing to her.

I put my hand to his chest, but then passively slid it around his shoulders.

Her eyes flickered, and it took all I had in me to ignore it and pull this little asshole against me.

"He's having a good time," I told her, and then shrugged. "Just be easy."

He grinned at me, then her, and the urge to clock him tugged at my fist settled on his shoulder.

He tipped his chin at her. "Yeah, be easy, Andie."

Honestly, I had no idea what I was doing, but when her face fell, I think I accidentally accomplished it.

Her hand went around his bicep. "Tucker, please..."

"Hey, um, *Andie*, is it?"

Her eyes went hard at me again, but I had never been ignored so quickly. She tugged at Tucker again, but this time, he pulled away from her. He looked to come at her with something again, but I asked him to take a sec, to get a drink and breathe, and surprisingly? He did.

Flashing Andie a look, he fist bumped me, then turned and grabbed his women. Together, they headed toward the bar, and I had to block Andie with my body to keep her from going after him. One thing I noticed, though? She wouldn't let my hands go anywhere near her, not this time.

Her jaw worked.

"Get out of my way." But no, I wouldn't be doing that, and she discovered that when I held my positioning.

I geared myself up for the worst. I pretty much knew she

could take me down where I stood, considering what I had witnessed ten minutes earlier.

Taking a step back, she laughed. It was a cynical one, though. No humor at all.

She crossed her arms over her chest. "What is this? You're my brother's new best friend now?"

Her brother! He's her brother.

That explained a lot a guess.

She went to step around me, but I blocked her again. Her shoulders tensed and I lifted my hands.

"No threat. I just want to talk."

Her eyes narrowed. "Well, I don't want to talk to you. And, is this your house?" she said, taking a step back to gaze around. "Where are your women?"

I had that coming.

Sighing, I pushed my hands into my pockets. "That night was a mistake. I was actually there to—"

"Make a deposit," she interrupted, making my brow twitch up again.

She nodded.

"I know everything that goes on in my club," she went on.

Her club? Well, damn she was really the wrong person to piss off then.

I'm such a fuck up.

I drew my hand down my face. "Look. Andie."

Her face twisted up at the use of her name.

I pushed past it. "What happened was a huge mistake. I really was just there to make the deposit. Things got out of hand and..."

But she wasn't listening to me.

She was watching Tucker.

Over at the bar, the kid was taking drinks from his girls, which had the woman in front of me wanting to do nothing but rip each one away from him. And that? That got me another idea.

No matter how much of a d-bag it made me.

"You give me back my reservation at the club, and I'll get Tucker to leave."

It was a chance I was taking, I admit that. But it proved to be the right one.

She shot me a quite intimidating glare. She had given the "Ass Grabber" a very similar look earlier. But this? This made that look like child's play.

She stepped up to me again, like she had the night she kicked me out of her club, and gazed up at me.

I followed every varying shade of brown in her eyes as she did. Each color was wrapped up in the other, twisting and turning, like they couldn't get enough of each other. Like they *had* to be together.

Her hand went to my chest, and I watched it, her finger touching right at my heart.

"Come to the club at noon tomorrow," she said, but then one more thing as she stabbed it into my chest.

"And stay the hell away from my brother."

Five

ANDIE

"WHAT WERE YOU *THINKING*?" I snapped, tossing a look over to the passenger seat.

What I found wasn't shocking.

Gazing out the window, my brother wasn't listening to me at all.

He never listened to me.

A breath expelled from my chest as I gripped the steering wheel of my Mercedes. I had to fight him to get him in the car, and leave all that bullshit at that house. He didn't need any girls right now. He needed to keep his head on straight and focus on what got him those girls in the first place, his game.

I huffed.

"Underage drinking, really?" I asked. He'd clearly put some away even before I arrived. He'd been stepping all over himself when I found him.

My acknowledgement of his behavior went again disregarded. His hands tucked under his arms, his eyes closing like he was going to sleep, and that only frustrated me more. It hurt me more.

A pang hit my chest as we traveled under traffic lights - the other street lights like fireflies in the DC air.

"You've got two strikes already, Tuck," I said, reminding him. He technically had three alcohol related offenses, but that last one had been thrown out. We had a lenient judge that day. She'd been from the old neighborhood. I faced him again.

"You trying to lose it all?"

He'd worked so hard for his success on the basketball court. I had worked so hard to make sure he could, and I'd do it again. I was happy to. I'd spent years dancing in clubs, putting it all away so he could go to those basketball camps, so he could shine when those scouts came calling. They eventually did, and now he was one of the most promising athletes in the game, but he could still lose it all. So quickly.

I finally got his eyes this time, though they were more than hard, and equally unfeeling in their stare. He stared at me that way a lot. I seemed to get it more and more no matter what I did.

"What I do," he said, putting his hand to his chest, "is no concern of yours. Hasn't been for a while, so you need to back off me, and my life."

That pang hit my chest again. It destroyed me that he felt that way. That he still felt that way after all these years.

I worked my hands on the wheel.

"I can't do that," I said, shaking my head. "I won't. You can refuse my help. You can run from the security detail I assign you, and get into as much trouble as you want, but I'm still going to be here. I'm still going to take care of you."

He was my brother. He was my only family, and I loved him.

The very words caused an expression I'd seen many times before. What I'd said twisted him up, a mashup of emotions flooding his face before it always settled on one. That one hit the harshest - the cruelest.

His gaze cut to me.

"You lost any fucks I could give you years ago, but do what you want if it makes you feel better."

I lost him again after that, but in my heart, I knew he'd been gone years ago.

And it was all my fault that he had.

I walked into a dark, lonely house after I dropped my brother off at his home that night. I lived in a high-rise downtown. I put in many years of working my ass off so I could. My place wasn't far from my brother's. I liked it better that way, though of course he didn't.

Tossing my keys on the end table, I found myself in the living room.

Not too much later, I made my way to a dark bedroom with a bottle in my hands. I'd never been one to self-medicate. But tonight had been hard.

I let the brown liquid burn away everything, the searing inside my chest and the thoughts in my head. I even thought about calling Tuck. I just wanted to talk to him. I just... wanted him to not hate me anymore. But why shouldn't he?

I hated me.

The bottle hit my end table, and I pulled out a drawer.

The picture was the only one I had of us not in a tabloid or on the front of a magazine.

Thanks to my brother's recklessness, I'd always been purposely placed in the background, just to make sure things went off without a hitch. But in this picture, we were together. We were together because both of us wanted to be, not just me. He was young then, like ten, to my sixteen, and even then he had a basketball in his hands. Situated under his arm, he stood long enough for me to get a picture of us. Our foster mom had taken it, the last one before I left him. Though I guess neither one of us knew it that day, or maybe we would have taken more together. I would have made sure we had.

On my right were the dark fingers of another person - the person responsible for why this picture had been ripped on my left side to omit them out of it. In reality, that should be a reason to destroy this photo, but it was the only one I had. It was the only picture both Tuck and I had before everything changed.

Ignoring the hand, I focused on what was important in this photo, brushing my fingers over the two of us.

Smiling, I placed it in my lap before reaching into the drawer again. My fingers found the chain, and the moonlight in the room caught the metal charm as I lifted it up.

He hated when I wore this thing, which was why it was rare when I did. But I would today. I needed it today.

I got the pendant around my neck; a shiny metal flower embedded in the work. Its weight was a reminder that things hadn't always been so bad between my brother and I. A little boy once gave this to his sister for Christmas, and maybe one day, he would remember why he did.

Six

D

THIS PLACE LOOKED SO different with the lights on, the quote end quote *average* lounge area, or whatever.

I pushed my hands into my pockets, flanking the tiny little thing escorting me around in a pinstripe suit. But I guess everyone was tiny to my six foot five.

"You'll have full access to the Onyx Room, and its subrooms," she said, waving to the entrance of both.

I nodded, moving on quickly, for many reasons. The first, because I knew Griffin wouldn't need much of a report of that area—the sub-rooms. My boy Griff, in his college days, would have been more than game for use of a secret room. But the married Griffin Chandler wasn't having it. He told me he'd taken his friend Taylor up on his suggestion for *Club Prestige* for its privacy, if anything else. There'd be a few dozen celebrities coming in for Ryan's bash and we'd need it. Being discrete was always best in the type of business we were in. The second reason, was the obvious.

The last time I'd been in the sub-rooms I was getting thrown out.

Katelyn, the girl showing me around, made sure the entire

set up was to my liking. They'd themed the room with dark couches and other handsome furnishings – very masculine, suited well for a *grown man's* event. Though it had been just the other night, the whole set up was very mature, and Ryan would like it fine. Katelyn also told me about security they had planned for us, and the very word had my chest dancing on the inside.

Where was Andie in all this? Would she be coming out? But as Katelyn took out her key, escorted us out of the room, and locked up, I knew she wouldn't be.

She handed me the key.

"A master to all the rooms. Each of your guests will receive one on check in. No one else will have access besides our staff."

I slid it into my pocket, nodding. After I did, I did something, well... kind of stupid.

"Is Andie around?" I asked, rubbing my hand over the back of my head.

I said it was stupid.

Katelyn's eyes narrowed, which made sense. I mean, what reason would I have for bugging Andie? What reason did I have for *wanting* Andie?

I had no answers for any of my questions.

"Ms. Simmons?" she said, placing her hands in front of her suit, "she's in her office. Did you need her?"

Did I need her? No, not particularly. But did I want to talk to her? Yeah, I kind of did.

"I need to pay the rest of my deposit," I said, realizing quickly that I did. I shrugged casually.

"She's an owner, right?"

Seven

ANDIE

"Ms. Simmons? Diendre Combs is here to see you. He has an event set for—"

"This weekend," I finished more than aware of the fact, and even more than agitated.

What does he want?

Chanel's sharp intake of breath could be heard even through my office intercom. She'd buzzed me as she was my administrative assistant.

"Of course you knew. I'm sorry," she hurried, no doubt believing my agitation rested with her, from how she sounded. She knew I was well aware of every event at the club - if anything, for security purposes.

Though, this clearly wasn't the case in this situation.

She breathed.

"But he is here and he'd like to speak with you. He's brought the rest of his deposit for the event."

My fingers played at my lips. He could have given that to any one of my assistants. I placed him with Katelyn, and she was more than sufficient. She'd worked here since we opened.

I pressed my finger to my phone's intercom.

"Tell Mr. Combs he can leave it with you."

Silence, and then a ping before her voice.

"He's requested drop off with you, ma'am. He wanted to speak with an owner."

But why?

My agitation quickly brewed into anger. I more than abided by his terms. He wanted his spot back, and he got it. He must want to play more games.

Well, I was the wrong girl to cross.

"Let him in." My finger lifted from the speaker, and I stood, coming around my desk. But I quickly realized he wasn't worth standing for.

Taking my seat again, I went into busying myself with schedules, and that's what I was doing as he came him; the click of the door alerting me to his presence.

Pretending to care, I glanced up, his long back to me. He was busy closing the door, and at full height, he rose well above my door frame. He took up even more of the room when he turned around.

Brown eyes lifted to me, and I kept them, watching him come over in a Polo tee, and the slightest sag to his jeans. They hung right at his hips, the gold plated belt keeping them up.

"Hey," he said, bringing his hands together. He had something in them, an envelope. He came forward.

"Thanks for, uh, seeing me."

My lashes flickered toward my desk, doing more of that busying. I picked up an agenda I'd probably read about three times.

"Of course," I said to him, not even looking up. "Is the Onyx Room to your liking?"

He said nothing at first, then, "Yeah, more than."

"Good," I gave him a quick glance, remembering the envelope. "I'm told you wanted to pay your deposit."

He blinked like he forgot the reason he came in. With

one stretch of his arm, he crossed the width of my desk despite the fact he was still standing a couple of feet in front of it.

"Yes," he said, handing the envelope over, "and thank you - for giving me the spot back."

Like I had a choice. But I took the envelope, hoping to end this encounter soon. Though he gave me the envelope and stepped back, he didn't leave. He simply brought his hands together, moving long fingers in and out of each other, and that did nothing but annoy me more.

And then he spoke, and made it worse.

"Andie—"

"Mr. Combs needs an escort," I said, my finger on my intercom, "he's paid his deposit and I'd like to make sure he gets to where he needs to go, okay?"

He blinked, but I did nothing.

"Of course, Ms. Simmons," Chanel responded, chipper like her usual demeanor. "I'll have Mason come up to escort him immediately."

"Excellent." I pulled back, staring up at my unwanted guest. I gestured toward the door. "You can wait for Mason outside my office. He'll make sure you don't get lost on your way out."

I wasn't backing down on this. I didn't want him here, but apparently he wasn't backing down either.

He folded large arms over his chest, his eyes narrowed, maybe even hardened. After a beat, he sighed though, dropping his arms to his sides. "I just wanted to apologize."

"And see, here I thought you already did that," I said, laughing a little. I folded my fingers across my stomach. "Remember? At the party last night? Or maybe you're apologizing for using my brother to get to me, and allow you back in my club? I'm confused, so I'm gonna need you to fill me in."

He pushed a large hand over his close cut hair after I said that, his gold watch reflecting off the fluorescents in my office.

He huffed. "That was fucked up of me. I know, and I don't normally do shit like that."

I nodded, my lips turned down. "So fucking two girls at the same time in a public place *is* something you do? I'm sorry. I just want to be clear on who exactly you are before I have my guy get you out of my office."

His eyes averted that time, his arms coming down to his sides, and I think I got my answer. The thing is, I don't think I needed to ask the question. That's how guys like him are. Give a guy a little power and they used it over others. It didn't matter if they were a celebrity or not.

That's something I knew all too well.

He pushed his hands into his pockets. "I didn't mean to disrespect you. What happened downstairs was a mistake and I really meant that last night. It was shitty and it shouldn't have happened."

"You're right," I told him, standing. "It shouldn't have, but it did, and because of you, I had to fire someone. Though, I'm sure that means nothing to you. Someone in your position doesn't have much need for an hourly paycheck."

A cold look casted my way, and it had been so quick that it threw me a little.

He went stiff. "I didn't always have money."

But he did now, and really, that's all that mattered.

I gestured to the door. "You know the way."

I half expected him to fight me more. He had since he violated my space, but he did turn around, and once he did, I could finally breathe.

Gathering my papers up, I actually did start on my work, but then I heard his voice again.

"Do you like flowers, Andie?" he asked, and my gaze shot

up. He was still at the door, his hand on the knob with his back to me, and my hand lifted too.

It touched my necklace, the silver one my brother had given me so long ago. It had a flower on it, a metal one with a small stone in the middle.

Had he seen it?

He didn't wait for my response, simply turned his head over his shoulder, and a small smile shone in the corner of his mouth.

"If so, you should get out to *Marigold's*. They're so pretty there."

He turned the knob the same time my phone rang. My cell this time, and not my office line.

My fingers left my charm, and I picked it up.

"Andie." My standard greeting was default to me, and it wasn't until after I said it that I realized I never checked who called. I went to do so, but then, I didn't need to.

"Andie? Where are you now?"

An eyebrow shifted, then two. It was my brother. It was Tuck.

"Tuck, um," I paused, swiveling in my chair a little, "I'm at the club. At my desk rather. What's going on?"

"At the club? Can you get here? Can you get to my house?"

Normally, calls from my brother didn't sound this way. They were more forceful. He needed a car to pick him up. He needed security to escort him to an event. But they never sounded tense.

And never, ever sounded scared.

"What's going on, Tuck?"

"The, uh, the cops are here, Andie. They're in my place and they won't leave."

My eyebrows narrowed, and then went hard. "The cops? Why? What did you do?"

In the background, I heard voices, official ones, and I was already reaching into my desk and grabbing my purse.

"They're asking me questions, And."

And... He never called me that.

"They stopped by and—"

"Don't answer any of them until I get there." I gathered my bag, sliding it over my shoulder. "Okay? You shouldn't be doing that anyway without a lawyer present."

"Okay. You're coming, though?"

He sounded like that little boy, my little brother again.

I closed my eyes. "Yes, I'm coming. Just give me a few minutes."

After he told me he understood, and after I felt secure in the fact he did, I hung up, then buzzed the front, asking Chanel to get the valet to bring my car around. But then, I hit a road block.

"I would, Ms. Simmons," she said with a lob in her throat.

"But, uh, you had me send it for an oil change this afternoon."

Of all the days...

"Can you have a car come for me then?" I said, trying not to snip. We got cars for our clients all the time.

"Yes, yes, I can do that. But it will be at least forty five minutes. I just had one called for Ruby. She also had work done on her car this afternoon, and the normal company we use is pretty backed up today."

Ruby. She was another one of our owners who actually took care of most of our legal stuff. I could use her right now.

God, Tuck what did you do...?

I pressed my hand to my brow, feeling nothing but sticky sweat as I turned in my chair.

"Can you call another charter? I really need a ride. It's Tuck. He's—"

"Can I help?"

My lashes flickered up, my head in my hands. Diondre had his hand away from the knob now, his lengthy fingers pushing against his palm.

What is he still doing here?

"I can, Ms. Simmons," pinged Chanel's voice into the room, "but it will take me a few minutes to track something down—"

I lost her at some point. I think it was that dark gaze ahead, the one that fastened to me in the strongest way. His sneakers brought him closer to me, his hand pushing into his jean pocket.

"Andie? Do you need help? A ride somewhere?"

I did need help... which was the only reason I said yes.

Eight

D

I HAD her in my car, one creamy brown leg crossed over the other. She didn't face me, her elbow on the window of the Ferrari I rented for my time in DC. Behind her dark shades, Andie gazed at everything but me, as we weaved through the crowded DC streets - and weave we did. There'd been urgency in her voice during her call; I felt I had to help.

I tried not to watch her, but my vision just kept navigating that way. She filled my damn car up even though I'd rented this one specifically to accommodate my size. Her presence clouded me, though it wasn't the soft, feminine curves that kept my attention this time. Her nails brushing under her chin, had me worried. They kept brushing. Her leg kept shaking and I felt like I was witnessing a sight not many got to see. I noticed something similar the night of the party, the night with Tuck. There was a crack forming on her tough exterior, her armor falling apart in front of me with every minute it took me to drive to Tucker's house. That's where she told me to go.

"We're close?" I asked, though I knew we were. The GPS kept us on track. I guess I... I just wanted to talk to her.

"Close," she said, trying not to look at me. Her amber skin glowed in the sunlight as she lifted her head back toward the window. I watched those fingers brush the underside of her chin again. There went that crack again, and I quickly realized that crack was Tuck. He was Andie's weakness.

He was her kryptonite.

A frenzy met us at the gate of Tucker's house, and I'd wished I didn't send my security on their way. They'd accompanied me to the club, driving behind my car as I went there this afternoon, but with Andie, I didn't want them around. I didn't know why. I just didn't need them, or want them, for some reason. I supposed I just wanted it to be the two of us.

The frenzy was in the form of paparazzi. They stood outside an iron gate, and I guess I understood why. Behind that closure were the cops. At least three squad cars parked up a long driveway. I had to navigate strategically just to avoid the photographers. It wasn't like I gave a crap about them, but there was clearly a scandal going on here today, and I had my fair share of them in my career already.

"I'm having them buzz us in," Andie mentioned, though she still wasn't looking at me. "The security. They're going to let us in."

She had her phone in her hand, speaking lightly to someone.

Calm, her leg dropped, then crossed the other way. If I didn't know any better, all this, the cops, the cameras, did nothing to faze her. But it was those fingers, those nails that gave her away. They brushed a ruby lip this time, after she'd put her phone away.

I drove faster, gunning it the minute the gates opened. We got the usual fanfare, the paparazzi redirecting their attention. A yellow Ferrari probably indicated someone important to them, and the tint to the windows would only argue that point more. The darkened windows kept them from invading our privacy, and I took us up the driveway to Tuck's house.

And boy did this motherfucker have a house. It was three stories—a colossus of unnecessary prestige. He probably didn't visit half of it, but, like most in the business I was in, felt they needed it. I supposed I used to feel that way, too.

I just had a mama that checked my ass.

My digs were simple in Chi-Town, and that suited me okay. I had enough, and I had a place for my mom and sisters not far from me. We had enough.

I was barely in park before Andie left my ride, slamming the door and rushing toward the entryway tucked in the back behind the house. And she did rush, her heels clacking against the ground.

I hustled with her, and ended up beating her to the door. Well, I did play basketball for a living. We met resistance at the door - an officer who liked to throw his weight around, but all Andie had to do was introduce herself, and her purpose, and he let us by.

I nodded, not trying to get mixed up with the law, if I could help it, and followed behind her.

The inside of the house matched the outside, large walls filled with artwork and classy shit the kid probably didn't pick out. It surrounded the home though, made it shiny and pretty. The living room kept up the standard. Cream couches took up a third of the room.

A kid in a bright orange jersey sat in the middle of it, one hand on his face, the other in his lap. Tuck sat in front of a cold fireplace, two other officers chatting off to the side with their hands on their hips. I didn't fail to notice how close those hands were to their holsters - their guns.

And neither did Tuck. He kept looking up at them, frowning before turning away. He wrestled his hands in his lap and this was a new kid in front of me. He was different from the one I was introduced to the other night, the cocky one.

He was very much a kid now.

And that proved at the sight of his sister.

He stood immediately, taking a step toward the door. They all did, him, the cops, when they spotted Andie come, then me. And that's where everyone's gaze flashed first, Andie, then myself. The cops... Tuck...

That's when Tuck stopped stepping. Something flashed behind his eyes.

His gaze left me and settled on Andie. It *narrowed* on Andie.

His chin went up, and he was back on the couch, hands in his lap like he wasn't just sitting in a ball of nerves minutes prior.

Andie's bag fell from her shoulder. "Tuck... What?"

He pushed his arms back behind the couch. "Took you long enough."

What was this D-bag's problem?

I palmed my keys, coming beside Andie. I got a grin from the douche and a wave of his hand as he said, "What's happening, D?"

I eyed him, but made myself engage.

"Nothing, kid," I said. "I heard you were into something. Your sister needed a ride over, so I drove her. I was at the club making a deposit."

That's when he stood, bypassing Andie entirely. He reached for my hand. "Good looking out, man. Thanks for being cool."

I wasn't cool, not with him, anyway. I made the shake short, standing back.

Andie pulled her shades off, and that directed Tuck's attention. It went to her neck, and his eyes turned to slits.

Turning away, he made Andie blink, and her hand came

up, her fingers settling on that necklace around her throat for some reason.

She dropped her hand to her side with a huff.

"What is going on?" she asked, and when Tuck didn't look any closer to telling her, the officers did.

One came forward, trying to look all official and shit.

"Andie Simmons? Your brother said you were coming. He wouldn't speak to us until you did."

She nodded. "That's me. What's this about?"

From there, the officer gestured toward the cop waiting in the wings. That one in particular kept his eyes on me, watching, for some reason. I couldn't say that was something that hadn't happened to me before, especially coming up in the south side of Chicago. A guy like me always managed to catch the eye of the cops down there. But this one was blatant about it, coming over and handing the other officer some pictures.

That cop handed them to Andie.

"We picked these up in a bust last night," he said.

Her eyes leaving her brother, Andie fanned through the photos. Her gaze sharpened, narrowing.

"Guns?" she asked, looking up.

But from over her shoulder, more than guns could be seen in her hands. That was a straight militia she had there, ready for battle with all the arms in the photos.

The officer nodded. "We got a tip about them. The perps we took them off outed your brother. Said he sold them to them just last night."

A curse flew in the air, and Tuck turned on his heel. And damn was that the wrong thing to do, the exclamation was more than incriminating.

"Impossible," Andie said, forcing her gaze away from her brother. And no nerves were present now. This was Andie. Serious, professional Andie.

"He was with me last night."

"All night?" asked the officer. "Because we have sources that put him somewhere else around two in the morning."

That passed over Andie's tanned cheeks. She couldn't deny it with the flutter of her lashes. They flickered over to Tuck, then her expression more than fell.

"Tucker?" she questioned.

She got a simple shrug in response, not surprising from the tool bag. He was where this officer said he was. I'd bet money on it.

The officer's colleague took the photos back, and again wasn't shy about staring at me. I really hated that shit. I had no issues with cops when they did their fucking job. But when they did this stuff, and were so blatant about it? I hated that.

He went to walk away, but stopped, and I went tense when he got all up in my space, pulling, of all things, a pen, from his shirt pocket.

He produced a paper after that, something that looked to be a receipt.

He grinned at me. "Can you sign something for me? My son follows Indiana. He'd love it."

I blinked. This guy was... a fan.

"Sure..." I said, not really believing this shit was happening right now. But it could be worse I supposed. I put on a smile, taking the pen and paper. "What's his name?"

"Brian, and are they going to get you more playing time? Because, man, when you're out there, you shine."

I think I was starting to like this guy. I smiled wide, and even wider when he let me use his shoulder to sign. "I haven't heard much about the new season, but I hope so."

"Yeah? That would be great. They'd be stupid not to."

I had only finished the signature when of all things the other officer shoved more stuff in my face, a notebook this time.

"Mine's for Henry and Jason. My sons," he said, and I laughed, not believing this at all.

I wasn't the only one.

Andie stood, jaw slacked with her bag nearly on the floor. Quite a turn, this all took. I finished the other signature quickly, both officers admiring my name like I handed them the most precious treasure. With a clearing of their throats though, they got back into this, and the officer, the more hard-assed one, pressed his hands down on his pants, facing Tuck.

"Now, Mr. Simmons—"

"Was with me last night," shot out of my mouth, and so did eyes my way, many eyes.

What the hell am I doing?

"With you, Mr. Combs?" asked the officer.

"With me, yes. And it's Diondre. D to my friends, so feel free."

That made this grown man's actual cheeks redden. He shook it off, again clearing his throat.

"But we received word Mr. Simmons was—"

"That was just a tip," said the other officer, putting his hand on his colleague's arm.

"Just a loose one." He faced me. "People put all kinds of names out when they don't want to get in trouble. We see it all the time, D."

I nodded. "Well, that must have been the case. Andie was with him some of the night, but the rest of it he was with me. We bounced around at some parties. And, nothing illegal, I assure you."

"Of course not," said the officer snorting. He *snorted* when he chuckled. That throat cleared again.

"I guess we're done here for today. Come on, Douglas."

He waved his colleague on, but I held the pair, pressing a hand to their shoulders.

I grinned. "Thanks for your help today, officers. I'll have my people send some tickets over to you guys. For your sons, as well."

More excited chuckles and snorts. Escorting them away, I got their information with promises to see those tickets through, and even waited until they got into their squad cars. I waved like a proud papa at the door, letting out a relieved breath when they finally left.

"Just back the fuck off, Andie," is what I got to hear when I came back into the house and the scene there made me want to rip the limbs from the little fucker's body I just saved. He had a finger out, shot pointedly at the concerned sister before him, her hands on her chest.

"Tucker."

"Just back. The fuck. Off. I'm not your business. Haven't been for years, so don't pretend you care now."

The words blanched her, making that beautiful skin of her cheeks pale, then rose. They got so red. He pushed around her, coming over to me, and I didn't shake his hand this time. I refused to, and maybe he saw that because he kept his hands to himself.

"Thanks, D," he said, his gaze averting.

I could give him nothing but a light, "Mmmhmm" in response. I couldn't care less about this guy. In fact, I *didn't* care about this guy—at all.

I'm pretty sure I did this all for her.

He tipped a nod my way before leaving Andie and me alone in his beautiful living room. We stood that way for a while. Still. Quiet. Andie's red lip went into her mouth, and like in the car, she did anything but face me.

So I decided to go over to her.

"Hey, um," I started, but I didn't know what to say. What *did* a guy say to that? A brother treating a sister that way in front of a stranger.

Pulling her bag, her eyes fluttered away.

"Thanks for the ride. I can call a cab back to the club if you want to just take off."

That's it. That's all I got. I didn't want a thank you. Actually, I didn't know what I wanted. I just knew I didn't want that, this.

Nor did I want to see a girl this pretty, this strong, on the cusp of tears.

She hid them from me, putting her glasses on, and I didn't stare directly at her. I didn't want to make her uncomfortable.

I pushed my hands in my pockets. "It wasn't a problem. I wanted to help." And I did. I felt I had to almost, compelled. Maybe I just wanted to figure her out. She seemed so guarded despite how strong.

More silence between us, and I didn't settle for it this time.

"Are you okay—?"

"What do you want, D?" she asked, her cheeks red. "You act like such a, a..." She didn't finish, letting out a breath. "Why did you help?"

I shrugged, not knowing what to say to that.

But then this came out of my mouth.

"You."

Her... I said her, and *that* got her attention.

Those dark eyebrows raised above her frames, so high and nearly reaching the buzz of her hair. They lowered slowly, and she pulled her sunglasses off her face. She had such big eyes, like a doll - wide, brown, and beautiful. I watched that metal flower of hers again. It was big, too, and so detailed as it rested on her full chest.

Her fingers went to it, playing with the large petals. And she said something, something that surprised the hell out of me.

"You mentioned *Marigold's*," she said, a lump moving in

her throat, "you said it was pretty, but I... I've never heard of it."

She'd never heard of it, huh?

Well, we'd have to fix that.

Nine

ANDIE

"You coming, Andie?"

Have I lost... my mind?

I stared up at the eyes probing me, that deep, dark gaze awaiting answers - awaiting me. D stood on a high staircase, a long body that could only be dwarfed by the likes of that which ran behind him. The massive jet buzzed, gleaming in the DC sun. D stood atop its ramp almost innocently, grinning like he didn't have half a dozen humming planes on the tarmac surrounding him.

He popped his hands above his head, stretching out long arms as he held on to the top of the jet's doorframe.

"Time's a-wasting. *Marigold's* is waiting!"

I shifted on my peep-toed heels. "I never agreed to—" I clamped back the words, biting down a temper. "You never said this place required flying to."

"And you never asked," he said, coming back down the stairs. He landed on the tarmac, in front of me, and how this man towered. I was five eleven with my white heels on, but D, he had quite a few inches on that. His arms extended, that wingspan resting on the railings of the staircase. "You wanted to see *Marigold's,* and that's where we're going."

His fit body followed long arms and biceps; both with the tone and hardness of volcanic rock. He said I wanted to see *Marigold's.* But no, I was tricked. I was tricked into wanting to see it by this man, this man and his arms and, and... his eyes.

They danced my way.

"We'll be back before the day ends. I'm assuming you have things to do at the club, right?"

I nodded.

A deep dimple pierced his cheek. "And I wouldn't take you anywhere I couldn't come back from quickly. I do have an event coming up at that same club, remember?"

I had forgotten and I didn't forget things.

But one thing he said was correct. He wouldn't take me far. He fought too damn hard for that spot.

I unfastened my heels from the tarmac, stepping toward him, and that spread a smile on D's face. He let me pass in front of him, and I mounted the staircase, making my way inside the jet. I had been on birds such as this before. My brother traveled this way quite frequently, though I advised many times against it. He was quite new in his game, and the world could be fickle. Things could be taken away as quickly as obtained, especially if a player spent his money too frivolously in the beginning. Private jet use was expensive, and could easily be switched out for a cheaper way of traveling.

Another thing he never listened to me about.

I dropped my purse on a padded seat, turning. I didn't fail to miss chocolate brown eyes. They hummed a full rotation of my backside, unashamed, before finding my eyes. I should check him for that. I normally *would* check him for that, if my body wasn't jumping because of it, my core dancing. D made averting my eyes hard. Like I said, he was unashamed by what he was doing. He was expressing his enjoyment of something, his approval, and he wanted me to know. He only let go to give an attendant a drink order, asking me if I wanted one, too.

I sat demurely on an ivory seat. "Um, just water please."

"Water?" D asked, lifting an eyebrow, but there was humor in his voice, a smile on his lips.

I nodded, facing the attendant. "Water will be fine."

The man in a navy ensemble acknowledged my request with a head bob, then headed away, leaving the pair of us.

Sitting tight in my seat, I held my purse in my lap. I studied the interior of the bird because I had no idea what else to do.

"You comfortable over there, Andie?"

Not really. Could he tell?

"Just fine," I said, pushing an ankle behind the other. Hopefully this made me look more casual, less tense.

His amusement of the situation – of me - he had to push off his face. His hand moved over his mouth, his leg crossing at the knee. He dropped his fingers.

"You should come over here," he said, stating the words casually, "those seats suck. You'll be more comfortable."

Currently, his long body sat on a couch against the interior wall. I was in a tight seat, no matter how plushy, that resembled that of a commercial flight. It was also located on the *opposite* side of the plane, which was why I'd chosen it.

I settled my arms over my purse with a huff. "I know what you're doing."

"Uh huh," he said, lowering his chin. "What's that exactly?"

The attendant came back, handing him a long neck beer. He took it, thanking him and I did the same when my water arrived ahead of me.

I placed the white napkin on my lap, setting the drink down.

"I may have entertained this whole... thing," I said, looking up at the plane. "But we should get something clear."

"What's that?"

"I did *not* come to sleep with you. I'm not one of your groupies, or... or your jump offs. I'm not one of your whores, Diondre."

I said them because I felt those words needed to be said. In all actuality, I had no idea why I had been entertaining this little endeavor. Something about yesterday, about the way he helped my brother - me, I supposed. But that didn't mean he could get anything he wanted from me.

Thoughts flashed back after that; the club, and how I found him. Was I becoming one of those girls? His playthings? How easily I'd come on this trip when he offered.

D had smiled nearly this whole time thus far, the whole day from picking me up to dropping us off at the airport, but that seemed to fade now. Yes, it was gone completely now.

His fingers moved to his jaw, pushing under his chin. He dropped his leg from his knee, leaning forward.

"Well, I guess now that we both completely understand why I *didn't* ask you to come out with me today, can you come over here please? It really is more comfortable, and the TV," he paused, gesturing to the center aisle above, "comes right down from the center there. I figured we'd watch some movies on the flight. You'll see it easier from over here, better."

Damnit.

He leaned back after that, settling in, and I got over myself for a moment, and decided to sit next to him.

We had a pretty short flight. And a quiet one. That had been my fault, but really, how could he blame me... considering the way we met.

The silence was filled with the drinking of beverages and chewing of snacks aboard the flight. It had been smooth and easy, and the entertainment only aided that. The TV actually provided us with television, not movies. In our time in the air, the crew had *Sanford and Son* playing for us, everyone on the flight crew laughing lightly - everyone but Diondre and me on that comfy couch.

Again, I guess I had been to blame.

The wheels hit the tarmac with a soft thud, the landing more than smooth in the luxury vehicle. Upon coasting, D and I remained silent once more, and I considered asking if we could just stay on the plane. After refueling and maintenance, we could just take off again, get back in the air, and head back to DC like nothing happened.

D unbuckled before I could throw out the proposition.

The crack of the door let the light in, and I unstrapped and got up, too. He was at the door now, looking out.

We need to just go back.

I pressed down my white shorts, straightening myself out after the hours in the air. D didn't watch me this time, and I was glad. He just stared out the door, his gaze wondering. He pushed off, and I lost him to the day, my frustrations looming. He was making this difficult. I swiped my purse off the seat and chased him out, chased him down the stairwell.

That's when a sight met me down at the bottom. It was a car, a beautiful shiny one like the car he drove in DC. It sparkled in the bright sun, and behind it was an airport, vast and wide. I had never seen it before in person, but I'd heard of it. It was hard not to know what airport it was, considering the landscape behind it.

Many buildings towered in different levels, and even from here, one of the tallest buildings in the world could be seen - it's steeple off in the distance and high in the sun.

I approached a man then, one standing in front of a bright

red convertible. He had his hand on the door, waiting patiently for me to take it all in. The city landscape laid behind him.

I pushed my hands in my pockets, tipping my chin to the vast city.

"Chicago?" I asked. I knew it well, though I'd never been. I booked my brother flights out here all the time. That's how I was familiar with the airport.

D's buzzed head lowered a little, and that smile returned faint on his lips. He rubbed his mouth.

"Yeah. *Marigold's* is here. My hometown."

His hometown. He took me home.

"I play for Indiana, but I commute from here," he went on. "I guess I couldn't really leave."

The door of the car cracked, creaking when he opened it, and I slid in. I went with him.

His hand on the wheel, D left the jet behind, as well as his security. We had a couple on the flight, though they remained scarce. I wanted to ask why. Usually these men, men like D, felt they needed to have security ready at all times. It made them feel secure I think, important.

He really was surprising me.

I popped my sunglasses on. The sun was so bright there, high and lovely. The breeze passed over my trim level of hair, and I caught D looking at me again.

Though this time, he pretended not to.

Clearing his throat, he moved his hand on the wheel.

"You ever been?" he asked, glancing at me. "To the city?"

I shook my head, my arm resting on the door.

I popped my chin on my fingers. "Can't say that I have, but I feel like I know it. I plan all my brother's trips when he comes."

The interstate met us at our entry into the city, and D nodded, taking us there with quick acceleration. He weaved in and out of traffic seamlessly. He knew these roads. These were *his* roads.

He glanced my way again. "Mind if I ask you a question, Andie?"

Andie.

He made my name sound different for some reason, or maybe it was just my ears.

I shifted in my seat. "Depends. Will I want to smack you after?"

That had him chuckling again, deep and thick. He pushed a hand over his head. "Possibly. But I'm willing to chance it if you're willing to answer."

Brave, this one, wasn't he?

I folded my arms over my chest, my attention his. When he noticed that, he went on.

"Your brother," he said, surprising me, and also making my heart race. He eyed me. "What's his deal?"

"Deal?"

He nodded. "Yeah, it just... it seems like he has one. One with you in particular for some reason."

He picked up on something he had no business inquiring about, but had to have noticed in all he'd seen recently. My drama with my brother was like a freight train, slow to take off, but deadly in the end with its speed.

I said nothing, turning away.

"Ask me anything else," I said, pushing my glasses up.

"Anything?"

Anything was better than where we were.

"How did you become owner of the club? Security?"

I smiled, why was this easier to answer? Maybe because that background felt more cosmetic to me, safe.

"I used to be a stripper." And when his eyes bugged out, I continued, laughing. "Not at the club, but in a past life. And there, I met friends. Together we started the club."

Club Prestige's beginnings had been a whirlwind, but the fallout had only been a successful business and lifelong friends. I met a couple of the owners through dancing, and at that time, that money put Tuck through all his training for basketball. He went to the best camps money could buy. His potential in his game was spotted early. It was actually his coach at the YMCA that discovered him, and suggested further training. Tuck said he wanted to, that he loved the game, so I made it happen any way I could.

Things had been rough for a while when I danced, no luxuries for me, but it had all been worth it. I wanted Tuck to have everything he could possibly have. I felt I owed him that.

I touched my necklace, fingering the pendant. In the end, it all worked out. My time at the club dancing found me colleagues, fellow dancers who hated the system as much as I had - the abuse of a male-centric management. Those men let all kinds of things happen to girls, horrible things, and in a more than dangerous environment. So, when some of my friends said we had a means out, I took it. We had a silent benefactor, another friend who had her own reasons for wanting to start the business, and well, *Club Prestige* was born.

"That's a hell of a come up," D said, taking me out of my thoughts.

I turned.

"From me being a stripper?" I asked, because that's how it sounded.

"In a sense," he said, "but I mostly meant you hustling, not backing down until you got what you wanted. That had to take some drive, right? Starting a business?"

He meant me being an entrepreneur.

I chewed my lip. "Yeah... yes."

He smiled a little, going back to the road.

"Same goes..." I paused, unsure if I wanted to get personal, but in the end, I pushed it down. I went on. "You got a similar thing going too though, right? You said you weren't always rich."

His eyes found mine, crinkling a little at the sides.

"Nah, I wasn't," he said, facing the road. "We both got something in common then, huh?"

I let the world surround me after that. I let *his* world of urban buildings and concrete fences take me in. We went right to the heart of the city, the environment, the air; completely different from DC. Both cities had their unique elements of people and places. It wasn't until we cruised for a bit and turned into a park that I realized we were staying right down here. A park - a wide abyss of leafy green sectioned off from the grey towers of city.

"A park?" I asked him, and D nodded, moving the wheel.

"*Marigold's,*" he simply said, and I wondered.

"How so?" I figured *Marigold's* would be some kind of shop, a flower store maybe? So when we turned up in a vacant parking lot, I was more than confused. It was completely baron, and connected was a small blue enclosure, a wide box of glass with greenery inside.

D shut off the car, pausing only to flash his eyebrows up at me, before coming around and opening my door. I could have beat him to that, opening my door. But I chose not to.

He stood by, idle and waiting for me to take his side. And when he shut my door, I eyed him, feeling a bit out of sorts. Where were we?

I pushed my bag up my arm. "I thought you said we were going to—"

"*Marigold's,*" he said again, and he gestured this time, tilting his head for me to follow him, follow him to the box. I did though I felt a little leery. He told me something, and it didn't seem like he was delivering here.

We approached the box, and I couldn't really see too much inside. So much greenery covered the windows. Near the door handle was a plaque, the name *"Fairfield Nursery"* on the side of the building, and below that there were hours of operation, the time now more than a few hours after close. Pushing my arms over my chest, I simply got another one of those eyebrow dances. When D followed my gaze up from the plaque, he grinned.

"Fairfield Nursery," he said, pushing his keys around. From the abyss, he found a long key, a round one with a metal flower embedded into the handle. He lifted it.

"Or 'Marigold's' as known by the locals."

The key he had let us in, and that whoosh of greenery filled the air around us. D guided his hand behind me, leading me in, and I stepped, making my way. My heels sunk a bit into the sod, but his hands went around me, onto my shoulders.

"Careful," D said, that grip subtle yet firm to my body. His hands moved down my arms, assisting me onto a cobblestone walk, and a slow, burning sensation made its way, traveling deep into my limbs.

I moved my arms around my purse, and he released me.

"Thanks," I said.

"No problem." His hands pushed into his pockets, and he tipped his chin up. "What do you think?"

In all his handling, all his touching, I hadn't taken the place in, and I wondered rather quickly how that had been possible. This place...

Flowers were planted into that same sod I sunk into. The area was surrounded in it. The little cobblestone paths looped and weaved through what were feet upon feet of colorful plants, and even more vibrant flowers. They hung from the walls, vines growing up them, and in the middle was a shallow pond, tadpoles playing at the sides of their dirt enclosure.

That made me smile, how in a way, they were kind of cute. That brought that smile to D's face, too.

He waved. "C'mon. I promised you flowers."

I didn't understand as there were literally flowers everywhere, but I understood rather quickly upon where he brought me. These flowers made the others look like insignificant weeds.

He brought me to sunflowers, massive in their size. The heads were quite literally as big as miniature umbrellas, and the petals as bright as sun kissed oranges. I'd *never* seen sunflowers so big, and I was sure D picked up on that pretty quickly.

He draped his arm over a shovel lodged in the dirt.

"Sweet, right?"

"Right." I reached out, touching one. The petals moved between my fingertips, deep in their gold coloring.

"They're my mom's," he said, then laughed a little when I blinked. He put his hands on the shovel handle. "Actually all of these are. She planted everything."

All of this? She planted *all* of this. But there was so many, flowers, plants in nearly endless rows.

"She did it all? Everything?"

"Yeah. Well, the start of it. Before it all grew." He gazed up, vision surrounded like mine. "The park left this place to run down, and wanted to get rid of it, but my mom wasn't having it. She took care of it, and the city ended up making it a nature preserve. People come from miles just to see the flowers."

I could see why. They were so beautiful. Especially, the sunflowers. It was hard not to get drawn in by them, by everything.

Leaning in, I smelled them. That's something my necklace didn't have, that wonderful smell that woke up the senses. When I rose, I caught D looking at me again. But this time, it wasn't at my body. He was looking at me, that enthralling, all-encompassing gaze.

"Don't let him fool you, girl."

The both of us turned, breaking whatever connection was

had over the pretty flower bursts. What broke it brought the widest smile out on D's full lips. A woman came around, a black woman, older, and holding a watering can. She had the handle over the area just above where an aged wrist might be. I say might, because her arm stopped right there, an area of taught, scarred skin that rounded, and smoothed out at the tip.

She eyed D under busy grey eyebrows. "This boy planted just as many of these flowers with his mama and sisters. He's just lying on ya."

The words had a sour expression forming over D's lips, but the way they went tight before relaxing let me know he was fighting it. In the end, he gave up entirely, bringing his entire wingspan around a woman who barely came up to his waist.

"Thanks for that, Ms. Gracie," he said, squeezing her. He simply gobbled her up in his size, his arm resting across the tops of her shoulders when he rose to full height. He gazed down at her.

"Lying on her, huh?"

"Mmmhmm, straight lyin'." A poke to his chest went with each word, her watering can sloshing on her arm.

She faced me. "Boy was here nearly every day with his mama, knee down in the dirt just as she was."

D's eyes lifted to the heavens.

"Needed something to do after basketball practice," he mused, but that smile on his lips told of that lie, too. This woman knew this man too well, clearly.

He gestured toward me. "Ms. Gracie, this is—"

"Andie." My error called upon me immediately. Not only were my hands left empty of one to shake, as Ms. Gracie's single hand was busy helping her hold the watering can, but my face was also hot with both her eyes and D's on me.

I closed my fingers. "I'm sorry I..."

Ms. Gracie batted a hand at me, then used it to help tip her can - the handle still over her amputated arm. From the spout, a fresh stream of water came down on calla lilies, and a grin sprang to this woman's face.

"Dear, don't you be awkward around it," she said, referring to her hand as she moved to water more flowers. "Haven't had this thing for years. Don't bother me none, so don't let it bother you."

I could respect that.

"Anyway, nice to meet you," she went on, then frowned at D. "And what you doing around these parts? Ain't calling no one, and then creeping up in my business unannounced. You probably was going to sneak through here wasn't you? And not say a dang word before you left?"

By the look on D's face, that theory rang true, his guilt placing a crooked smile on his lips.

He squeezed Gracie's shoulder. "Didn't mean anything by it, Ms. Gracie."

"Mmmhmm," she said, her lips turning down. But she couldn't stop that smile. "It's a good thing I wanted to get a few more things done after close, otherwise I would have missed you."

"Ms. Gracie is the groundskeeper here now. It's why the place looks the best it ever has."

D's words only widened that pleasant expression on Ms. Gracie's lips. She rose up after taking particular care of some sun kissed daffodils, dotting them with H20.

"I do what I can to keep it up, but your mama was the true artist. This place thrives whenever she comes through, though I understand her being busy. She's real active in the school board now, and the old neighborhood appreciates her for that."

The words Ms. Gracie passed over her shoulder, the pair of us following her while she did her last minute rounds. How those words played out on D's expression had me feeling some kind of way, the words about his mama. I rubbed my arm, trying not to think about them, be affected by them, but that was hard. It was so easy to place D in a box. He was a man, all visceral of his wants over his actual needs. He took what he wanted, and gave in to whatever he saw fit because he could, and I had seen that firsthand. That's how I met him. It was hard to think about Diondre the man, the human, who had a history and a family, one he clearly cared about deeply.

Ms. Gracie threw D a grin. "This place missed you, too, you know?"

He smoothed a hand down her small shoulder. "Been a little busy, I guess."

The statement bubbled light laughter; that grin ever strong on Ms. Gracie's mouth.

"Well, you stay busy. You stay makin' us proud." That got D modestly shaking his head, and Ms. Gracie reached back, squeezing his hand on her shoulder.

"I'll let you get back to your date. This old lady's got a little more busying to do as well before I take off for the night."

The word "date" immediately drove me to correct, but this Ms. Gracie was swift. She left us standing there with her words before flittering away and doing her busying, just like she said.

I rubbed my hands restlessly on the back of my shorts, and D did something similar. His long body rested back on a planted tree, arms crossing and uncrossing a few times. Moving near him, I reached out for some vinery, the silky leaves curling on the tree he rested on.

I smiled. "So you helped your mama after school, huh?"

That deep, throaty laugh came, making that massive chest rise and fall. And he watched me, my fingers, as they went down the vine.

"I liked to say I enjoyed it for what it was, but I got to see my mom. She worked a lot, so I popped in here for a reason to see her. When she wasn't at work, she spent a lot of time here. I think it meant something to her. My grandma used to work a lot in here too with her when she was younger."

He said "used to" in regards to his grandma. Thinking I understood that for what it was, I moved to another vine, and those brown eyes followed as well.

"Your mama still around here?"

His head bobbed once in acknowledgement. "Mmmhmm. And my house isn't far from theirs, she and my younger sisters. The girls are in high school now."

"Will we get to see them?" I asked surprising I think both him and myself. His brow twitched up, curious, and I corrected quickly, pushing a hand behind my neck. "I mean, Ms. Gracie was furious you almost rolled through here without seeing her. I could imagine doing the same to your mama would be World War III."

The response made me grateful for the correction, D passing my words off with another chuckle.

"You're right, but nah," he said. "They're in the Cayman's now."

"*The Cayman's*? As in, the Cayman Islands?"

"Yep," he went on, pushing off the tree. "Finally got my mama to go on vacation. I sent her and my sisters there for a few weeks."

Of course he did. Because that's something someone would do when they cared about people they loved. I reached for another vine, and again, D watched me do it. But the leaves fell when he took a step forward, getting closer to me. He got so close, a hair's breath from my body, and just a touch from even more.

"Can I feed you?" he asked, pushing his hands deep into his jean pockets. He smiled a little. "Something quick, and then I can take you back - take you home."

Home, yes. I needed to go home. I had a job to do.

A click of a lock moments later, and we were at the start of the journey back to DC, the nursery's door closing behind us. D fiddled with that, getting it locked, and I stepped away. I needed to step away. I needed to breathe. On that quest for air, I stumbled across concrete ahead. It had a few wide holes in it and the cement that formed them was a damp, deep grey.

I frowned.

"It must have rained while we were inside," I said, heading over. I got in the center and that's when I got D's attention.

His head whipped around. "Andie, that's not—!"

The wave of water shot straight up, and a force of sharp current went right into the underside of my shorts. Just as quickly as it happened, it stopped. The waves moved on, the current making a "follow the leader" procession onward down the concrete lane of holes in the sidewalk.

I honestly was frozen right where I stood, and very much afraid to look at the damage. I knew exactly what color my shorts were, and any underwear I owned would show right through it.

D made it to me quickly, his face a mashup of shock and humor. Though he tried to hide the latter. His face went overly stiff, his hand rubbing behind his neck. "That's not rain."

"I got that." The water dripped down to my heels now, and as the day was dwindling down a nice crisp chill was hitting my nether region.

He reached out for me, then thought better of it, pulling back. "Come on. Let's get you a—"

His words cut off by the water that hit him, and it got him good, too. It shot right between his legs.

I know because I pushed him right over it. I couldn't help it really. I was wet. I was uncomfortable, and well... it seemed like fun.

His hands snapped right over his junk, rubbing a little, but that shock didn't last as long as mine had when he stared me down. Something dark settled upon his eyes, eyebrows descending like storm clouds. And when they flickered to the right, on the trail of water coming right at us, I knew what was next.

I ran. I ran for my life, a feat I knew impossible. I had a basketball player behind me with limbs only too long. They swiped me up quickly, and he tugged, pulling me into a jet of water that soaked us both. Heads, shoulders, toes. All white was see-thru, and my red drawers only on display through my shorts and the white strips of my top. But for some reason, I didn't care. For some reason, I laughed.

D laughed too, his navy t-shirt sticking to him and clinging to every ridge, every bump of muscled surface under-neath it. It brought his biceps out, his shoulders like rock slabs, and his eyes... His eyelashes collected each drop of water, making them clumpy, errant beads following to his lips. They fell into his mouth, and then they fell into mine.

He kissed me...

He gathered me up, his hands on my shorts, his mass hitting my heat when he pressed me into him. He didn't do it on purpose. He was just so large, so big... *everywhere.* My hands to his cheeks, I wanted that burn below, that heat and not just from his mouth. He went hard before me, more rock, more him. His hands on my wet shorts allowed him to grind, allowed me to grind... on him.

A sharp tug went to my lips from his teeth and I decided something. And I think it was that same something that brought me here. I wanted him.

And I think I wanted him for a very long time.

Ten

ANDIE

Everything was wet, our clothes, D's car, me. He took me to his home, an all-brick colonial style with a two-car garage. It was all very subdued, quaint, and completely without excitement, or flare. It was comfortable.

It was home.

The walk to his bedroom was one of urgency, flesh and limbs. He wanted my body and I wanted his, neither of us questioning the other. This went beyond our bargain; no sex just spending time together, and even though, I think we both fully understood that didn't matter. We were two grown ass people, and at least for me, I was going to do whatever I wanted. I wanted D's body. I wanted him.

And I was going to have him.

He affixed his mouth to mine, delicious flesh revealing when he reached, pulling up his shirt. We both pushed it off and to the floor, a body of iron plains greeting me in more than a friendly manor. Diondre Combs was a basketball player. He trained his body for performance, so perfection was much of a given. But the hardened dips and rises of his abs was something of an outlier. He was marble, a polished work of obsidian tone.

He peeled my shirt off, his fingers running along damp skin. My bra had turned translucent, everything had - so nothing was of a mystery to him. His fingers to my shorts, he pressed my breasts against him, his hand shoving down and reaching for my core.

Sharp breaths escaped my lips and flowed into his mouth, his fingers a maddening dance of fluent strokes, and soft strums to my bud. Fresh juices tingled around my sensitive lips, as well as coated his fingers. My shorts and wet panties fell to the floor and I stepped out of them, jumping.

He caught me like he was meant to, like he was always meant to. I gripped around an unwavering body, the smell of heady flesh so near to my nose. I tasted his neck, biting, and a groan pushed from his body and went clear into mine. We fell together, a tumble of lust and body. A snap of my bra and he had his mouth on my breast, using his teeth against my diamond hard peak. He was so rough before he was gentle, but then so soft when he was kissing them, loving them.

He caressed, massaged, using his mouth to warm and suckle. He laved, pushing those long fingers into me ten-fold. He used two, then three using my cream to take me deeper.

I gasped.

"D…"

Any cries only made him go harder, faster. He drove his fingers like a piston, making my hips flutter up, and off the bed. A sharp rip showed a broken condom wrapper in his teeth, and before I knew it, his pants were down, thighs the size of thick tree trunks surrounding the most beautiful cock.

He pumped it rising up and taking the condom out of his mouth, and that had been the first time I saw it. He had a question in his eyes, something there that made him stop.

I rose to my knees, kissing him. He had a smell so fine, but so thick like sweet molasses. I felt his hand between us, his large mass, then suddenly, he grabbed my hips, moving up to my waist.

He forced my back to the bed, pushing my legs apart. Whatever had him hesitating before, seemed to have left him. He surrounded me with his body, grabbing the headboard, and those eyes welcomed me in at an easy thrust. It was all too easy, too easy for him to take me.

He pierced, jabbing like a heavyweight. He went deep, his extended length allowing him to take him there, to take *me* there.

I fingered his body, reaching up to cup large shoulder blades. Bringing him down to me - his charged body amped up in explosive thrusts. His body was frantic, powerful, and primal, but his lips? They told another story.

His mouth opened and closed on me, so soft to the touch on my neck, and when they touched my chin, then took my mouth - I forgot myself. I forgot my need for his body. I forgot all desire for his heat, and touch. I just wanted this, his mouth moving over mine like a sweet song. And it was sweet. His body knew how to make me come, but his mouth?

It knew how to love.

He took me there, his cock fast and merciless, but the real high came from his lips on mine, my body a shallow pool of raw emotions.

Gasping, I held his body and he held mine, taking me as he pushed his hand over my cheek. I drenched around him, legs shaking and everything else in a rapid quake. We were both so wet, damp from the fountains and sweaty from the sex. We were completely clammy and...

It was amazing.

∽

"What happened to um... to Ms. Gracie's hand?"

We'd been talking for what seemed like hours, the sun high in the afternoon. We talked about many things; his life on the team, my life at the club, but those things had all been cosmetic. Occupations had always been safe, good topics.

He brought his hand down my side, resting it lightly on my hip. He brushed his lips over the shell of my ear, and I laughed. That's why he did it. He had done this a few times now.

"A house fire," he said, smoothing his mouth on my cheek. "It was in the old neighborhood. The one I grew up in. The houses there were shit, and some faulty wiring took hers up one day. We were next door neighbors with her."

That settled like a mass, a hard stone in my chest. "Where were you guys?"

"At school." He paused to bring both arms around me, "my mom at work. Could have been us, too. The side of the house my sisters' rooms were on got blasted just as hard. God was really looking down on us."

How true that was. Wow.

I drew my nails down his back and smiled when a small shudder quaked through his body. I kissed his chest. "We grew up in a similar place, my brother and I."

He lay still, body warming at the kisses to his pecs.

He smoothed his lips on my head. "Yeah?"

"Mmmhmm. We both grew up in the system, foster kids."

All light topics, all safety, had clearly gone out the window now, and I think he knew that. He was oh so quiet, and this man never ceased to have something to say.

I pulled my hand from behind his back, burying my face in him. "And that's the answer to your question. It happened then."

"What?"

My face was hidden now, completely lost in his smell. "My

brother's deal. You asked what it was. Well, his deal was there. It was with me."

A warm finger drew down my cheek, brushing down to my shoulder. He wouldn't push me on this. Maybe that's why I kept on.

"I thought I was in love," I told him. I pressed my body into him, his arms pulling me closer, harder. "Our foster brother - and people found out, his parents."

I left out the part where he coerced me, bathed me in attention and love I never had before. He set me up to want him, and it wasn't until later I wondered how many had come both before and after me. It was him I ripped out of the picture of my brother and me. I did the moment I was no longer chasing his high. It was the moment I grew up.

I shrugged. "When it all came down, I was taken away and placed in a group home. Tuck and I were separated for *years* until I was able to get out of the system, then work up enough income to take care of him. And he... well, he's never forgiven me for that."

My fingers played at my necklace, the metal pendant he gave me before that final Christmas. It was D who slid it from my fingers, studying it. I smiled.

"He gave it to me. Tucker. He did before it all came crashing down. It's the last gift he gave. I tried to make up for leaving him, being selfish. I put him through all the best basketball camps growing up, and to this day, I try to do what I can for him, but... it never seems like it's enough."

I didn't know why I was telling him all this. I shouldn't be telling him this. But I did, and it was done.

Again, that big body of his kept the silence. Then suddenly, I got a nod, his fingers handing my pendant back to me. An embrace of Diondre Combs's wide limbs followed.

"I almost lost all of this before I got it," he said, raising his eyes to the room. He reached down tracing the shell of my ear, but I didn't laugh this time. Even though it tickled, I didn't laugh. He was so serious this time, no laughter or smiles allowed.

"I did some stupid shit in college," he said, "got caught up in some illegal betting with some powerful people and almost took my friend down with me. He was completely innocent in it all, everything going on around him. It was fucked."

"Oh my God."

"Yeah."

"What happened?"

"A damn miracle. It was actually him who was responsible for getting me out of everything. Him and his now wife, and we're still friends, Griff and me. I don't know how we are after all that, but he's still one of the best friends I've ever had."

I thought about that, so confused by the fact.

So I asked him.

"Why do you think that is? That he forgave you? That you're still friends with him?"

I didn't know why I asked. I guess that's what happens when you open the door, when things stop being safe, when things are real.

Diondre smiled at me, those teeth so white and bright. He had the best smile. I think I could watch that smile for so very long.

He bent, kissing my nose, but once he did, he stayed there.

"I guess he felt I was worthy of forgiveness," he said. "Even if I didn't feel I was."

Eleven

D

THE EVENT COORDINATORS had the Onyx Room looking hot tonight, but I knew it was Andie. Andie had *Club Prestige* looking awesome, and I couldn't thank her enough. The entire place looked like a tailored suit. Classy, with its dark tones and warm light. The music had the place hopping, and all my friends, and all Ryan's boys, we here. We made sure of that, Griff and I. Our friend, and old college roommate deserved it. He enjoyed playing for Canada, something he'd told Griffin and me several times. But that was Ryan's personality. He wasn't a complainer. He took the opportunities bestowed upon him, and that's what made his new offer so great. He'd finally been traded to DC. He finally got to come home.

He hung out by the piano player, super stoked that we'd all come out for him, that we'd put this together for him. Griffin arranged for a car to have him delivered here from the airport, and Ryan... well, this kid did all but shed tears. I think the support and thought got to him or something, but Griffin and I slapped him out of all that emotion. Ryan had been bouncing around since then, making his rounds to see all the people who'd come out for him. I hoped he'd take advantage of the side rooms set up for him at one point, though. They were all open to live dances for anyone who wanted it, keeping the main part of the Onyx Room more of a club experience with a few dancers' silhouettes only visible through a white wall near the piano player. Only their forms could be seen behind the smoked glass, and Griffin had set it up that way. Tonight, this place was more about the party, the social aspect, more than emphasis on the stripping, and I think that had been purposeful on Griff's part. Doing things this way would make himself and others who were tied down like he was more comfortable. But I found myself not disagreeing with that like I thought I would. In fact, I didn't think I would be using those private rooms myself tonight. I didn't have any desire to.

Smiling, I tipped back my scotch, looking for her. For Andie. I hadn't seen her at all tonight, and actually, not since I dropped her off at her house yesterday. We got in pretty late, but that was okay. She worked at a place whose normal business hours were purposely late, so she hadn't been too upset by that. She hadn't been upset really at all yesterday, and I might even wager by saying she had a little fun. She enjoyed her time with me.

She wasn't the only one.

A hand moved around my shoulders, taking me out of my search for the girl who I knew could more than kick my ass.

But I definitely wouldn't mind the tussle.

Instead of whom I had actually hoped for, I got Griff. He grabbed my hand and then I got him in a sweep, a strong hug. I hadn't gotten to see him tonight, though I knew he'd been poking around somewhere. He threw this party, both of us did.

Teeth nearly as big as mine shown under his blond hair. Though, I was sure my dark skin brought mine out more, especially with these club lights. He slapped my back, wearing a suit that *almost* looked as good as mine.

Almost.

He grinned. "I see you came through. Got the place back for us."

And Christ if I hadn't. Who knew what he'd do to my ass at another blunder. I was counting my blessings with this guy every damn day.

I laughed, shaking my head with disbelief that I actually had been able to do it. Get this place back. "I didn't want the alternative—i.e. you kicking my ass."

His bark of a laugh exploded over the club noise. "I'd say you made a good decision. And Ryan looks like he's having fun."

That was the goal.

He caught our eye, reaching up to wave in the pinstripe thing he had going on. I couldn't do stripes, but our boy could pull it off.

I brought Griffin down by his shoulders.

"How's married life?" I asked. "The honeymoon?"

I knew him to have flown in directly from Miami early this morning, Fiji right before that.

His mouth lifted in the corner, that smile going wide and I'd wager that had to do with his little woman.

He shook his head. "Do you really want to know? I know you hate talking about that stuff - settling down."

My vision caught Andie then, and when I caught her, I caught her. A short black dress encased the most feminine form, tight curves. That along with her heels and red lipstick, one would think she was a dancer, or server, not one of the most badass chicks in the building. She had her tanks with her, Gorilla One and Gorilla Two, but that didn't bother me. They knew their place with her, and if anything, backed her up, and that made them nothing but okay with me.

Griff turned, eyes fleeting that way though he had no idea who I was looking at.

I smiled.

"I do," I said tilting my glass, "but I can imagine the usual, though. Sex, sex, and more fucking—"

"Yeah. Won't be talking about that with you, but yes, we had a good time." He shook his head, taking a swig from the long neck bottle in his hands.

"We did things different," he went on. "Getting married then waiting a bit for the honeymoon. But I'm glad we did. It gave us some time to get things in order, Roxie enrolled in school and all."

That's right. She was doing the continued school thing, law school.

"And she doesn't mind you being here?" This was still a strip club, though I damn well knew Griffin Chandler wouldn't be partaking in the festivities. Like I said before, he was different now, not the college guy I used to know.

A smile moved across his lips. "Would you believe me if I said this was actually her idea? She hangs with Taylor's wife. Apparently the two make a thing of coming down here on occasion, a couple's retreat."

Sounded right up my alley. Ironically enough, it just might be, what with Andie and all. I mean, she did own this club.

"Roxie and Celeste, Taylor's wife, got to talking about my plans for Ryan," Griff went on. "I was at odds at what to do, since I wasn't from around here. That's when Celeste threw out the club and Roxie passed the idea on to me."

I really wasn't surprised by this from the woman he'd married. Roxie, well, she had always been pretty cool. Actually, cool didn't define it. She saved my ass once upon a time with that betting scandal, though I knew a lot of that had to do with Griffin. And on top of it all, the two had trust. They trusted each other. They had no reason not to.

And I was sure the love only helped that.

I smiled, happy my boy had found that. He deserved nothing less.

"So what's next?" I asked. "Babies and what not?"

My best friend went flush, though he hid it, rubbing at the tint on his face.

"Someday, yeah. Someday."

I bet this guy would load her up. He came from a big family, a whole brood down in Texas, and I knew Griffin to be a family man. He always was. Thoughts of that life always kind of passed over my head, but when he talked about it, it didn't seem so bad.

Especially if one day I had *her*.

Andie found me, found us. She'd sent her gorillas away at this point, but I doubted they were far. They always looked out for her.

But I had her now, and I went for it, reaching for the back of her arm. She came with a curious smile, and I surprised her by a casual side kiss to the cheek. She was working, and I understood that.

I could tell she appreciated that, that smile going wide on her lips.

"Are you having a good time, Mr. Combs?" she asked, and that grin on her lips went knowing.

I settled my hand on the small of her back. Not saying to hell with appropriate, but *definitely* letting her know something.

"Fabulous time," I gestured toward Griff. "Have you met my boy? Griffin—"

"Chandler," she said, finishing for me. She was good at that assertiveness, and I couldn't get enough of it. She reached out her hand, shaking his. "I spoke to you on the phone about this event. Andie Simmons."

"That's right," he drawled. He did have that country-ass accent after all. He smiled. "Nice to meet you, and thanks for forgiving this guy's stupidity and letting us back in. I really appreciate it."

My transgressions would continue to follow me, but he was right, thank goodness for Andie. Thank goodness for her forgiveness.

I hoped what he said wouldn't bring back old wounds with her, and relief hit when all I got was her hand around *my* back.

She rubbed. "I guess he's worth forgiving."

The double meaning I got immediately, and had me wanting to kiss this woman more than I already did.

"I hope you both continue to have a good time, and if you need anything, make sure to grab me or one of my people."

Griffin's gaze traveled then, from me to Andie, then back again. It might have had something to do with our hands, unashamedly holding each other.

If a twinkle didn't hit this guy's eyes.

"Thank you," he said, looking at me. "We really appreciate that. Everything really."

She nodded, sliding her hand away from me, but I grabbed it. When I did, I kissed it, just once but it was enough to, again, let her know something.

"I gotta go do my rounds. I'll see you later, though," she said, turning, and then she faded into the crowd, like the hottest chameleon on the block.

Unfastening my gaze from her, I brought my drink up, but paused knowing eyes were blasted in my direction. Griff had his hand on his chin, eyeing me but I could only ask him, "What?" before taking a drink. A suited woman crossed my vision who I hadn't seen since I paid my deposit. Her name was Katelyn, and I knew her to be one of Andie's security assistants.

I grabbed Griff's hand, bringing him in. "I'll catch you

later, 'aight? Got to speak to one of Andie's assistants about security things."

"Okay, stay easy."

"Stay easy."

I left my friend with a snap, and went on my way. Someone I hadn't seen yet should have been here by now, and Katelyn would know if he showed. She turned at the call of her name, smiling brightly.

"Can I help you, Mr. Combs?"

"Uh, yeah. There's a guest missing. I just wanted to know if they checked in yet."

She pulled a clipboard from under her arm. "Sure. The name?"

"Tucker Simmons." I invited him tonight, but not because I liked him or was particularly fond of him. Fact of the matter was, I despised the guy, but maybe if I spoke to him, I might not by the end of the evening. He seemed to listen to me, and maybe I could get through to him about Andie.

Their history didn't seem entirely fair, but even if she did leave him while in the system, she didn't deserve the way I'd seen him treat her. I knew it wasn't my place to talk to him about things that had nothing to do with me, but like I said, he seemed to have some kind of respect for me. Maybe because we were peers, so I wanted to try with him, and if it didn't pan out, Andie would be none the wiser. I highly doubted he'd talk to her about me approaching him. He seemed like he kept interactions to a minimum when it came to her.

My hands pushed into my pockets as Katelyn checked the list, and when she said Tuck hadn't checked in that sunk in my chest a little. But maybe he was just late. Maybe he'd still be coming. I sent word through my people to his, letting him know about the party filled with our colleagues who played throughout the country. I figured it would be a golden opportunity for him, and he'd jump on it.

Maybe I was wrong.

"Can I help you with anything else, Mr. Combs?"

I told Katelyn no, and then took it upon myself to scope out the party. He might not have made it to her updated list yet. Going with that, I tried to check around a bit. He might have been sitting away in one of the corners, or even in a private room. I wasn't going to check in there though.

For obvious reasons.

I had been so buried in my search I nearly crashed into a waitress. I told her "Excuse me," but then she grabbed me, and when she did, she didn't let go.

"Diondre," she said, smoothing a hand up my arm, and as I had no idea who she was, I said nothing but, "Hey."

Maybe she'd seen me on TV for something.

"Excuse me," I returned, but again, she didn't let go.

"Oh, poo. Don't act like you don't remember me."

She pouted her lips then, making them full, and I did remember her, and once I did...

I moved out of her hands, pressing mine down my suit. "Hey, um..."

"Tasha," she said, pushing a hand down my chest. She did that a lot that night. That's how she got me into a dance, and later on, a threesome. I had been more than willing to at the time, but things were different now. Things had changed, and being seen with one of the very women that got me kicked out of this place wouldn't be a good thing.

Especially, if I was spotted by the woman who kicked me out.

I gazed around, trying to find Andie. She didn't seem to be around though, possibly making her rounds like she said.

"What are you... uh," I started, clearing my throat a little. I faced her.

"What are you doing here?" I'd actually heard she'd been fired because of me.

Maybe she remembered that because her face fell, a frown forming on her lips when she crossed her arms.

"I was invited," she said, pulling a drink off one of the server's platters. I guess she wasn't a waitress like I originally thought. They wore completely different outfits, and not as scandalous as Tasha's lacy number. There were just so few women here tonight. This was a secular event—technically. It was just girls tended to not show up to things like this, letting their men have their fun.

"Who invited you?" I felt no shame in asking her. I needed to know who I could talk to about her, to get her out of here.

That really brought something out on her face, and if I didn't know any better, she was about three seconds from throwing her drink in mine. She thought better of it though, bringing it to her pink lips.

She swallowed. "Tucker Simmons actually. He said it was the place to be tonight."

Why wasn't I surprised? I invited the guy to come and he takes it upon himself to bring in more bodies. Classic tool.

Maybe I shouldn't talk to him about Andie.

"So..." Tasha said, not missing a beat. That hand went up my body again, my lapel this time, and I wasn't surprised she didn't back down after I was clearly uninterested. That's just how these types of girls were, too easy to take to bed, and even easier to treat like shit. She pointed to the side, toward the private rooms.

"Want to go have some alone time?" she asked, getting closer. "I don't work here anymore, but we can still have fun. I haven't forgotten how to have fun."

I was sure she hadn't. But my perception of fun had changed, or at least, was being interpreted differently now.

I left Tasha, declining again, and made a new mission to find Katelyn. She could get Tasha out of here, and she had to—now.

Twelve

ANDIE

I TIPPED my chin to a dancer in a teal wig, a new girl, and one I hadn't had much experience with. She performed in some of the other rooms at *Club Prestige*, but was quickly becoming a hot commodity, hence why she was in Onyx tonight for the man of the hour. This evening's event was for a recently recruited basketball player from Canada. He'd been traded to our home team, and these festivities were for him tonight. The new girl had been paid to take care of him, and from her small reputation, I'd say this patron would definitely have a good time.

I checked on him through one of the mirrors, waiting with his hands wrestling in front of him on a couch. He was nervous, and possibly a first timer at this, but the dancers always were good about getting guys out of any shyness.

The dancer waved at me, knowing exactly who I was, I imagined. Everyone did.

I watched her tan back fade into the room, then I let her do her thing, happy this was my last room to circulate for a while. I wanted to get back out on the Onyx floor. Yes, to make sure everything was okay, but also to check on a few other things... *people...*

I guess one in particular.

Smiling a little, I headed toward the exit of the back rooms, but a voice in my ear had me stopping mid-reach to the door.

"Andie? Ms. Simmons?"

Mason, my number one.

I pressed my fingers to my tiny earpiece. "Yes, Mason?"

"We have a disturbance in room three, and as she's female, I thought it best to call you."

He knew I preferred to handle escorting out females. I trusted my men to not be heavy handed, but sometimes accidents did happen. Especially when women got too drunk. When we allowed rare secular events like tonight, confrontations were always possible. The women in particular could be very messy and I didn't want my men injured because they had to hold back while trying to maintain order.

I picked up my feet, rushing just a little as I didn't know how out of hand things were. "I'm on my way. Just keep her there until—"

"It's Tasha."

I nearly stumbled on the carpet. For just a second, I lost my thoughts, my footing. But once I got them back, I flew. Tasha. I had *fired* Tasha, and if she got in fully knowing I fired her... her purpose here wouldn't be for any good reasons.

How did she get in?

The door was open when I rounded a corner, and I fully expected chaos, a tussle of limbs and red hair— but what I got was a woman sitting pretty, and smug while she kicked back a drink.

That was until she saw me.

She lowered it, blinking, and Mason and Gerard, my

number two, stood in front of her with their arms crossed. That should have been enough. *They* should have been enough to let her know she wasn't staying here. It shouldn't have taken me.

I stepped in. "What are you doing here, Tasha?"

Her cool demeanor, though flustered at first, she got back, mocking confidence as she stood. She pulled her skirt, straightening it out.

"I was invited by a guest. I was waiting back here to give him a dance."

Like hell she was invited by a guest. I grabbed Mason's clipboard. "Who invited her?"

Scanning the list, I looked for her name. I had just found it, and began running over the line to who had put her on the list, when I heard a laugh, an obnoxious one, one that condescended.

I gazed up, and she'd gotten closer, though not much, as Mason had stepped in front of her.

I raised my hand, keeping him at bay. She wouldn't do anything. She'd be stupid to. I let my search go, and handing off the clipboard, I gave her the audience she clearly needed. I got close. I let her get close, moving my arms over my chest. "Do you have something to say to me?"

Her heels came to a stop in front of me, her lips curved up in a sly smile.

"Oh, I got plenty to say to you, *bitch*. But one is, I know the rules here. My name is on that list and you can't do anything unless I violate something, which I don't believe I have."

Technically, we could remove patrons for any reason, but the general consensus was we didn't, unless they did something wrong. It was bad form to do anything otherwise. She was testing me to act on the "whatever reason" policy.

"And my name is there. Right there," she went on,

pressing her finger haphazardly on Mason's clipboard. She grinned at me. "So have fun kicking me out."

I had seen her name on the list, which again, brought me to whom invited her. Deciding to get to the bottom of this *away* from her, I turned, gesturing my men to follow, and a giggly chuckle came from behind me.

"That's right, bitch," she shot, "and I'll tell him you said hi once I give him a good ass lap dance."

I turned on my heel. "Who?"

She winked. "Wouldn't you like to know?"

One swift motion and I got this girl up by her skinny, little arm. She squealed, and I got up in her face.

"Who?" I sneered. "*Who* are you giving a lap dance to? And *who* invited you here?"

This girl's mock confidence had completely evaporated now. She couldn't walk in here throwing her weight around, and I was going to show her a bitch if she continued acting a fool. *I* was an owner of this place and because of that the rules rang with me and my colleagues - not her. *I* was in charge and—

"A basketball player," she screeched, causing me to blink, as she'd said it so fast.

"W... What?" I jumbled.

She left my hands when I dropped her, falling to her knees. Her head lifted, her eyes slits. "A basketball player," she repeated. "Who obviously likes me more than you."

How could she know about D and... me? How could...

How could *he*?

But he had before.

I rushed from the room, but not before shooting back a few choice words.

"Get her the hell out of here," were the final words I'd be exchanging with that girl. She wasn't welcome here. Never again. I got down the hall before I heard clomping after me. It was clomping I didn't have time for. But Gerard said the only thing that could stop my haze of red.

"It's your bother," he said, and when I turned, he had his finger to his earpiece. He listened for a moment. He listened for a long time before pulling away slowly.

"Looks like he was just escorted out, too."

Why the *hell* was my brother here? Did he need something or...

Gerard was still listening to his earpiece. "Seems he got in a fight with a guest and security had no choice but to ask him to leave."

Since when did I not know what was going on in my club? I mean, I checked the list of guests for this event days ago and neither Tasha, nor my brother were on it.

"Why was my brother here? When did he get on the list? And who—?"

"Seems he was added this morning," Mason said, coming around Gerard. From behind them both, screams could be heard, and then Tasha appeared, her flailing body being lead out by two of my female security guards.

I gazed away.

"By who?" I asked. I needed to know who. I need to know who I needed to talk to, but then Mason checked his list again, said the patron's name and I...

I lost it.

I found Diondre in a dark place that night, and maybe, that had been ironic. I think I had been in a dark place with my original interactions with him, a vulnerable place. I had to have been if I let him get that close. I let him get his hooks in. I let him have a little piece of me fully knowing who he was, and how he was.

He'd been by himself in the Onyx those few moments later after my confrontation with Tasha. He was poking around, looking for something even, and when he spotted me, he made it seem like that poking was no longer needed. Like the sight of me concluded his search. He did that full grin he does, that sexy one that made his lips look so kissable, and all I could think was that I had to make that smile go away. I had to get rid of it, so it no longer... so it no longer affected me.

I just remember my arms flying, his hands grabbing my wrists. From somewhere behind, Mason, or was it Gerard, summoned me to stop, and from somewhere ahead, D's eyes begged me to. They all got me away somehow, and slowly, I discovered we were in the back rooms.

That's when my hands went back to D's chest. He stepped back, but I think only because he felt he was supposed to, not by any force of mine. Mason and Gerard were there too. They stood outside the dance room, their silhouettes visible through the door.

"How *dare* you?"

The words made D's eyes widen, even more than when I grabbed at him, pushed him. He rubbed a hand over his head. I pushed him again, and he once more got my wrists.

"You invited my brother? Really, D? For what reason? What reason could you possibly have? I told you to stay away from him. I told you not to fuck with him. I told you!"

I hadn't let a thing linger before I threw more out, and with each word, D's face fell. It fell completely, until he had understanding.

He lowered my wrists, and letting go, he rubbed his hands.

"I can explain, Andie."

Explain. He could explain.

I stepped away, and he reached grabbing me.

"I didn't invite him for me," he said, "or to have a fucking good time. I invited him for you."

I whipped around, pulling my arm back. "What?"

"You." He gestured toward me.

"For you. If you haven't noticed, your brother treats you

like shit, Andie. He treats you horribly, and it's not warranted at all. I thought if I could just invite... If I could talk to him... He seems to listen to me."

"He seems to listen to *you*," I snapped, "you who has it all together. You Mr. King of the Fuck Ups."

He cringed a little when I said that, but didn't stand down.

"Yes," he said, nodding. "I just thought I could talk to him. You don't deserve how he treats you. You've done so much for him, and still do."

"And what place is it of yours to step in? To think you need to fix my family?"

"It's not. I just wanted to help."

"Help, huh?" I pushed my hand behind my neck. "And while Tucker and me are getting that therapy session on, what would you be doing? Or should I say *who*? Tasha? After all, you did invite her. Was that your plan? Keep me preoccupied with Tucker while you go have your fun?"

His eyes went wide. "What? No! Fuck, no. Andie—"

I can't believe I'm so stupid.

"This," I said, raising my hand up and down toward him, "whatever *this* was is done."

"Andie!"

I left the room, spotting my boys immediately, and they were my boys, completely loyal. I told Gerard to make sure D didn't follow me, then asked Mason, too.

"Where's my brother?" I asked, charging out into the main Onyx room. The party was still charged, as if nothing had ever happened, as if I hadn't lost it on D.

Mason followed. "We tried to have him escorted to your office, but he wasn't having it."

"Where is he now?"

Mason spoke, his fingers going to his earpiece. When they

left it, his eyes lifted to the ceiling. "He's on the street. Raising hell like he does."

Why does he do this? Continue to do this?

"I'm going after him," I threw behind me, "watch the club."

I took the elevators to our ground floor, the all-white of *Club Prestige's* waiting room greeting me. Our concierge, and overall gatekeeper, Will, acknowledged me with a nod, then I was out the door. Gazing around, I attempted to spot my brother.

I heard him before I saw him.

He was yelling down the street, clearly drunk, as he clomped down the lane outside the club, and he had something in his hands, something small and black that he waved around. It had a handle. He held its handle.

Oh my God.

I ran, cupping my mouth. "Tuck!" But he didn't hear me, he just kept walking, waving around what was in his hands.

"Tuck!"

As he was stumbling, I got to him quickly, and confirmed immediately what I saw down the street. He had a gun. One he wasn't shy about holding onto on a public street. A dance club was across the way, and they were watching his spectacle, his ranting, but from their distance, I had no idea if they could see what was in his hands. If they could, they might not still be waiting outside the club in such a formal line.

Tuck went to step off in the direction of the club, but I grabbed his arm. I went for the gun, but he wouldn't let me have it, sheltering it.

I patted the air, letting him know I was no longer trying to take it from him. "Tuck, what are you doing?"

His eyes were so hazy. This wasn't just alcohol. He used the gun to scratch his chin, shaking his head.

"They're going to pay," he said, "they're going to pay, And."

My heart squeezed at my shortened name, then sunk. I touched his shoulder, but he waved the gun a little again. I lifted my hands.

"Who?"

"Those assholes." He rocked now, swaying while he nursed the pistol. "I sold stuff to them, Andie. I sold them guns and they ratted me out to the cops. I know they did because they were talking shit about me at *Prestige*. They didn't even need to mention me. Their lawyers got them off, took care of them, but they ratted on me anyway. They used me, and were fucking bragging about it at your fucking club!"

I closed my eyes. That's what the fight had been about?

"Why did they do that, Andie?" he asked, his eyes glistening now. "Why did they use me when all I wanted... I... I just wanted them to... To like me."

The words absolutely crushed my heart, ripping me apart at the very core. I had never heard him speak this way, and if I had, it had been too long to remember. I wanted to console him, but he stepped back.

Rubbing those tears away, he raised his hand, then shook his gun at the club across the street. "They're in that club now. They went there after security kicked them out, and I'm going to make them pay."

A shot rang out, a sharp one, a loud one that sent down all the people in that very line. But it didn't come from my brother's gun, no because I was holding him.

He was tucked into me, hugging me. He dropped the gun long ago, in fear, in remorse I had no idea, but he held me, his fingers curled into my dress. He held me like a little boy and I held him, but the shot had us both seeking out the source. From ahead, three men came; three men who had their guns pointed our way.

"It's them," Tuck whispered. "It's them."

I had no idea what he was taking about. Just that in his journey for acceptance, my brother had made some enemies, and those were now mine. I pushed Tuck behind me, ready for anything. They wouldn't get him. They wouldn't get him unless they went through me.

Those first shots flew and I expected a burn, my body bent over my brother's, but that heat of impacted flesh I never felt. Instead, I smelled hot rubber, burning rubber. A flash of yellow crossed in ahead of Tucker and me, and a car took the brunt of the rapid shots.

I stood, both Tucker and me. In front of us, a yellow Ferrari had burned to a stop. It was a Ferrari I'd seen before. It was one I'd *been* in before, and what was in the front seat had me screaming. There was a body there.

Diondre's body was collapsed and sunk over the front seats.

D

THE PAIN WAS EXCRUCIATING, racking through my body like hot, liquid fire. I felt quite literally sliced at all angles, jabbed and pricked a million times over, and I didn't know how to make it through it, least of all how my body would.

In the back of my mind, I thought... how grateful. And I was grateful. I was lucky.

No one else had to be subjected to this crap but me.

Heart hurting, I stood behind the glass of a downtown car repair shop. The shop had a car, a beautiful car with a once glistening finish. That finish was gone now, its light extinguished like a firefly to a bug zapper.

That tended to happen when the finish got riddled with bullet holes.

A noise escaping my mouth, I continued to watch the yellow Ferrari's restoration, the sound nothing but my internal anguish at the scene. This was agony, pure agony having to watch this, but torturing myself, I stayed every minute. I felt I had to. I owed it to this once flawless ride. Lost in my despair, steps sounded to my right. They were soft steps, uneasy steps.

Tucker Simmons had a look on his face when he got to me

by the glass - a goofy one that I wanted to slap clear off sometimes, but I was getting used to it. I would get used to it... for his sister.

He chewed the corner of his lip, another one of those clown shirts nearly dragging down to his knees it was so long. He rubbed the back of his neck, moving in nearer to me.

"It'll be okay, D. It's not even your car, man."

The fool.

I shot my hand to the glass, the sparks of hard work shooting off the side of a gorgeous ride. They had to buff the damn thing out, the detailing crew. The Ferrari wasn't *my* ride, but I had rented it for *my* time in DC. That car was a treasure and because of *him,* it had bullet holes in it.

I frowned. So many words I wanted to say behind my lips, but I had a feeling no matter how many different ways I tried to say them, they wouldn't get through to this kid.

Biting them back, I turned to the glass again. I'd watched these guys for hours at the garage. They assured me they could get the job done right, and after they were finished, I fully intended to make the car my own. I had a history in it now. We bonded. I didn't go out of control with my money often, but when it came to exotic cars I had a soft spot.

Probably why Tuck wouldn't get it. He spent his money at the drop of a damn hat. I could tell by the size of his friggin' house. He probably barely set foot in half the rooms it was so big.

Those soft steps retreated as they did every time he tried to come over here and tell me how I should feel about this situation. But then they stopped, and when they did, a set of heels revealed themselves.

Andie came from the other waiting room. I knew because she was an active visitor near the shop's glass window with me.

Pushing an arm around Tucker, she rubbed his head. My jaw had nearly dropped the first time I'd seen her do that to him, but then it came up. It came up because not only did he let her, but smiled when she did.

That brought mine out as well.

"Don't worry about him," she said, trying to whisper the words to Tuck but I heard them. I always heard.

"He's gonna be all right," she said. "I swear."

"You sure, And?"

"I... I *think* so."

They didn't get it. Neither one of them did.

A sigh fell from my lips, and from my peripheral, a loud-ass shirt left. Tucker left. After he had, a hand came sliding up my chest.

I let Andie in, dropping my arm down on her shoulders. I never fought her, but I was losing more and more energy with every minute I was forced to watch the world behind the glass. It was tense and... heartbreaking.

"I don't know how I'm going to hold up," I said, shaking my head, and a light laugh fluttered in the air, then touched my cheek when she kissed it.

"Oh, you'll be okay. I told you we'll pay for it."

"It's not about the money, Andie." I told her this before. I faced the glass. "This is hard to watch."

My words went without a response, and I turned, seeing nothing but a smile on this woman's beautiful lips.

"How are you so damn cute?" she said, smoothing her hands up my chest. I let go of the glass. I was... distracted.

Those slender arms of hers looped around my neck and her breasts pressed against me, her wonderful, bountiful chest. I got to see a lot of it through her tight top, and even more of her through the cream skirt that wrapped around her ass like a taut rubber band.

"Must you continue with this show?" she asked, her fingers locking behind my neck. "Tuck already feels bad enough."

I grabbed her waist. "He should. He killed a car."

"The car is fine, but most importantly *you* are."

I jostled her hips a little, never too good with words. Especially when it came to ones like those, ones that showed her thoughts about me, ones that she cared.

"That was very brave what you did," she went on, smoothing her hand down my neck. "Those guys would have killed Tuck."

And her, too. She'd found out who they were. They'd been at my buddy's party that night, but were kicked out after a confrontation with Tuck and went to the club across the street. Tuck followed them there with every intention of clipping their asses, the fool. Anyway, they'd apparently heard about the ruckus he was creating and came out to finish him.

That's when I had come in. I got in my car after I'd found out Andie left. I had no idea how much distance she had on me, so naturally, I thought I needed wheels. But when I saw those guys... their guns...

I put the car in the crossfire, and it caught the hits long enough for the guys across the street to be taken down. I was just glad everyone was okay.

"I figured I'd be you guys's best chance," I admitted, smoothing my hands down her hips, "you might not have had one if I didn't." I took a gamble that night, and as it turned out, it had been the right one.

I lost her gaze then. It went away and through the glass, though I doubted she cared too much about the car. She already expressed that.

"You didn't have to do that," she said, her throat moving at the words, and I curled my finger under her chin, making her face me.

I smiled. "Since when do I ever ask permission to do anything?"

"You don't," she breathed, and with it, a small smile touched her lips. "Thank God you don't."

I rubbed her hip.

"So you talked to Tuck? You guys okay?" By okay, I didn't know what I meant. I just knew that he had been around me just as much as she did today, and each visit had been very much without aggression, and resembled very much a... human, a kid.

"We talked," she went on. "Also because of you."

"What can I say, I work miracles."

"I'm starting to believe it." Her head lowered, those brown eyes facing me when she lifted it. "And you're not King of the Fuck Ups."

"Actually... I am." I made her laugh when I moved her hips. I liked her laughter, so much. "But you love me anyway."

"Maybe... Maybe one day."

"Yeah?"

She chewed one of those red lips, pulling it in, and I tugged her chin, making her release it. If I could make this girl love me, make her see I was worth the love, that would be the ultimate happening, a true miracle I might not be worthy of but more than willing to take.

"Maybe one day soon." Her smile had me smiling.

I dropped my forehead to hers. "I'd like that."

"Yeah?"

"Mmmhmm. I feel like I already got the like part down. The love can only be right there on the wings."

She rubbed her forehead against mine.

"You think you're always right, don't you?"

"Not always," I told her lifting my head. "I just hope I am with you... this time."

Her arms sagged a little. "I'm sorry. About that girl, Tasha? I know you didn't invite her. Tuck told me he did and—"

"Don't talk about her. Just..." I wasn't good when it came

to things like this, but if I could just say the right words, if I could say them just once...

"Can we try this?" I asked her. "You and I? The two of us being a thing, I mean. I'd like to, Andie."

Her lashes flickered down a little. Her head popped up. "You just live so far away, D."

"It wouldn't matter if I lived in DC. I'm rarely at home because of my job."

"See that's the problem. You're so busy and—"

"I will always be. Probably for the rest of my career on the court, but people make it work every day. We take this slow, and see what happens. But we won't know anything unless we try, unless *you* try."

She really had all the cards here. I had no idea what the future would be for us, her here and me there, but one thing I did know was this could work. My good friend had one of the best relationships I had ever seen, and now, one of the happiest marriages.

Marriage... the word had me laughing inside, then smiling. *Where had that come from?*

"What?"

Caught, I let the expression fall a little, though not completely. I pressed my mouth to Andie's, for the first time in my life, ready to take that step, to take *any* step with someone else.

"I want it to work," she breathed, lost in our kiss, my lips. "I want to try."

It was good that she said that... because I had already started looking at second properties based in DC.

Call me *optimistic.*

Click the link below to download book five of The Found by You series!

Download on Amazon